In My Boxes & Breakups Era

Lola B. Marie

Paperback ISBN: 979-8-9986331-0-2

eBook ISBN: 979-8-9986331-1-9

Book Cover by Acacia @ Ever After Cover Designs.

Edited by Jaquelyn Vale, She Who Edits, LLC.

For inquiries, please contact **lola.b.marie.author@gmail.com.**

1st edition 2025

Contents

Also by

Lola B. Marie

A Soul Seen

"I can't stay long...I see you, Emery. Come back to me."

It was supposed to be a one-time weekend at a haunted hotel—a wild, carefree bachelorette party for her sister. But for Emery, it became much more.

She kept coming back, drawn to him. From the moment their souls brushed against each other, Emery felt a connection that defied reason. Every encounter was a whirlwind of passion, leaving her questioning the line between dreams and reality. She was falling for a man who appeared only in her dreams...but who felt all too real.

Now Emery faces an impossible choice: remain rooted in reality without him, or seek him forever in her dreams.

A Soul Seen is a fast-paced, seductive novella about love that transcends reality, where Emery must discover if the passion she's found with Patrick is worth chasing—or if their love is destined to remain a fleeting, ethereal connection.

Note From the Author

Content Warnings

This book is intended for adult readers (18+), as it contains explicit language and detailed sexual scenes. If any of the following make you uncomfortable, please proceed with caution or consider choosing a different book. Your mental health matters.

- Explicit Language
- Explicit Sexual Scenes
- Spousal Neglect
- Sexism
- Misogyny
- Heteronormative Gender Roles

To women. Women who think they're too much. Women who hide their sparkle to make others more comfortable. Women who never put themselves first. Women who are more than mothers, wives, daughters. Women who are learning, growing, searching. Women who find joy and choose to hold onto it. Women who stood up and said, "Enough!" Women who champion other women. Women who break molds and destroy generational chains. Women who are more than their trauma. To women. To us.

Part One

August

"I think the tiniest little thing can change the course of your day, which can change the course of your year, which can change who you are."
-Taylor Swift

Chapter 1

♥

*"So make the friendship bracelets;
take the moment and taste it."*

"Open *your own store'*, they said. *'It'll be fun'*, they said," I mumble to myself as I move items around on the display table for the twentieth time. *It never looks right.*

The bell over the door rings as Frankie's booming voice seems to echo around me. "The fun has arrived!"

I turn to see her standing in the entryway of the store, smiling at me. Her face falls slightly as she notices my tension. "What, you didn't like my Rosie O'Donnell impression? Tarzan? No?"

I don't have it in me to play along, so I close my eyes, pulling a deep breath into my lungs. I hear Frankie start to walk toward me but don't open my eyes until I feel her hands softly rest on my shoulders.

"Hey, stop freaking out. It's going to be SO fun. Now, where do you want me? What can I do?" She relocks the door before walking through the store to set her purse down inside my office. Her colorful tattoos are on full display under the black tank top she's wearing, and her dark hair flows in waves down her back. *This woman.* She's my champion. And she's been with me every step of the way in this journey. When I told her I wanted to open my own clothing boutique, she immediately started doing research and helped me figure out how to accomplish it. We've been best friends for five years since bonding at a toxic corporate job that we've both since left. And now we are here, the opening weekend of my store, All Eras. I decided to lean into my status as an adult Swifty and marketed my store as having something for everyone, no matter what era you're in.

"I don't even know. I think everything is ready, but my brain is bouncing from one thing to the next, and I can't decide on what actually needs to be done." *The ADHD is REAL today.*

Frankie walks to my side and places her hands on her hips. Looking around, she finally says, "I think it looks great, babe. Try to stop the overthinking. This opening is going to go so well. You've done everything to prepare. Now you just need to let it happen."

Frankie walks to the front windows to peer outside as I keep futzing with the items on this particular table. *It never looks right!*

"Where's Brad?"

I can feel her gaze burning a hole in the back of my head. I put a smile on my face so she will hear it in my answer. Without turning around, I say, "Golfing." The responding silence could strangle you. It's never good when my loudest friend is quiet. I sigh and turn to her, holding up my hand to stop whatever's on her lips to say. "Don't. It's fine."

"Don't? Are you serious? He's golfing instead of being here for your opening weekend? What the hell, Jo?" Her face is severe with her brows pulled together and her lips downturned. She's waiting for an answer, but I don't have one that she'll like.

I try to keep my voice upbeat, but she doesn't miss the fact that I avert my eyes as I respond. "You know it's easier this way. He would just get in the way. He doesn't get my mania anyway. You do. That's why you're here." I finally meet her eyes and give her a genuine smile. Her face melts into a softer version of concern.

My best friend doesn't love my husband, and it makes things...difficult...sometimes. We were already married when I met Frankie, and it didn't take long for her to express her disapproval of him and our marriage. Frankie seems to have popped out of her mother's womb with a giant backbone and an ability to voice her opinions to the world. She's a lot, and she owns it. The same cannot be said for me. And while I have worked very hard to stamp down my people-pleasing inclinations, I can't seem to tame them when it comes to Brad. I married a man who assumed I was someone that I am realizing I'm not. But he still expects the same woman he married. It's a balancing act that is getting harder and harder to perform.

A knock at the door startles me from my wandering thoughts. Frankie is already unlocking the front door to let Kay in. My face breaks into a smile upon seeing them.

"There she is! My sweet Josephine! It's the big day!" Kay walks over to me with a package under their arm and a signature pad in hand. "I was so glad when I saw your address on my list this morning. I wanted to be able to see the opening day!" They set the package on my front counter as I scrawl my name to sign for the delivery. Kay is the 58-year-old UPS driver that has my address on their route, and I've been seeing them a lot over the last few months as I've had countless deliveries getting ready to open. They've been cheering me on from the start, providing me a little ray of sunshine every time they come in.

"I'm glad you could see me before I lose my mind," I say. "I'm stressed." My shoulders ease a little as I let out a sigh. Frankie rounds the corner of my counter and comes to stand beside me, softly knocking her shoulder into mine in a silent sign of solidarity.

"Oh, honey, it's going to be fine! You've got your person here." They nod at Frankie. "And customers are going to flock in. Don't you worry." They tap their signature pad and smile as they head toward the front door. "See you soon, sweets!" They casually wave as they let the door close behind them.

"Dude, I love her." Frankie relocks the door as she stares out the window, where Kay is climbing back into their truck.

"Them. You love them." I correct Frankie's slip of the incorrect pronoun for Kay.

"Damn. Them. I love them. Thank you." She looks toward me. "Need anything? I can always run and grab anything you might need."

I let out a long breath. "No," I say quietly. Then I straighten my back and lift my chin. "I'm ready."

"That's the spirit," she replies with a wink. Then she runs back into my office and pulls a bottle of champagne out of her purse. I laugh out loud as she carefully pops it open. "I didn't bring any glasses, so we are drinkin' straight from the bottle." She holds the bottle in the air toward me. "To you. To putting aside your fears and doing the thing you've dreamed of doing. I'm so fucking proud of you. You don't even know."

I take the bottle from her and chug a giant gulp before handing it back to her. "I really did it, huh?"

She takes a drink from the bottle before responding, "You really did."

We each take another swig before she sets the bottle on the desk in the office. I walk to the front door, where I see cars starting to fill the parking lot. I turn back to Frankie. "Ready?"

"Bitch, please," she scoffs.

I laugh before flicking on the open sign and unlocking the door.

Chapter 2

♥

"I didn't opt in to be your odd man out."

I pull into the driveway, expecting to see Brad's car in the garage, but he's not home. *That's weird.* I left before he did this morning since his tee time wasn't until 11am, but I expected him to beat me home.

Opening day was...chaotic, in the very best way. Frankie and I barely had time to think; it was so busy. Happy tears fill my eyes as I think back on the last few hours and how amazing it was. I couldn't have asked for a better opening. Everyone who came in was so friendly and supportive. I can tell that some of them are going to be regulars, and I can't wait to get to know them. I loved being able to help pull sizes and styles for people as they shopped for new clothes to feel beautiful in. Frankie worked the front counter so that I could mingle and help customers on the floor. I dry my eyes as I finally climb out of the car and head inside.

I'm immediately hit with the sight of a dirty glass sitting in the middle of the kitchen table, next to a used napkin. The plate and fork at least made it to the counter *next* to the sink. Though why it couldn't have made it all the way into the sink baffles me. Sighing, I set my bag down and grab the glass and the napkin off the table. I throw the napkin in the trash and open the dishwasher to load the straggling dishes. My warm, happy bubble from the opening has popped.

I make my way to the bathroom so I can take a shower before changing into comfy clothes. I need to unwind from the excitement of the day. I light a lavender candle before turning the water on to heat up. Letting the soothing smell wash over me, I strip my clothes and toss them into my hamper before stepping into the shower. I make it halfway through my routine before I hear the bathroom door open.

"Hey, babe!" Brad yells over the sound of the water. "I had a pretty good round today. It was hot, but otherwise the weather was perfect." Before I realize what's happening, he's stepping in the shower with me. "Scooch over, I need some hot water."

I step into the cold air of the shower, out of the stream of water, before he finally looks at me. "How was your opening day?"

I force a smile onto my face. "It was great. I had a ton of people come in. And Frankie was a huge help."

He rolls his eyes at the mention of Frankie. "Well, I'm glad it went well, babe. I'll have to stop by and see it now that you're open. What's for dinner tonight?" He turns back to the hot water and starts pouring body wash onto his loofah. *Guess I'm done in here.*

"I hadn't thought about it. Didn't have much time to think about anything other than what was happening at the store." I step out of the shower, pulling a towel around my body.

"Yeah, but you've been home for a bit, right?" he calls through the shower door.

I sigh. "Can we just order something tonight? I don't feel like cooking."

His head pops around the fogged glass door. "Babe, we're down to one income. We really can't be spending money on takeout. You should have thought of this before you decided to quit your job and open a store that won't see profit for at least a year." His head pulls back inside the shower. All of that was said with a teasing lilt to his voice, but the words drip in condescension, and I don't know how to respond. I wrap the towel tighter around myself before finally saying, "I'll see what we have to throw together." I leave the bathroom before I can hear his response.

Chapter 3

♥

"I was enchanted to meet you."

The other side of the bed had gone cold in the amount of time I spent staring at the ceiling after Brad had gotten up to get ready for work. The last week since the opening passed the same as any other week, and I wondered why that felt so *wrong*. I didn't expect him to change who he was just because I was changing and growing. But I guess I was hoping for more outright support from my husband. More pride in what his wife has accomplished.

I finally drag myself out of bed to get ready to head to the store. But as I'm making breakfast, I can't help but reflect on the last 13 years.

Brad and I met our senior year of college. He was the handsome business major with a five-year plan. I was the wild child looking for a reason to settle down. In hindsight, I was only a wild child because I was rebelling against the strict religious background I was raised in. College helped me realize that I didn't share the same beliefs that my family did, and it caused a rift that has never been mended. Plus, as the firstborn child of four, I was held to a different standard and didn't receive the same unyielding support that my siblings did. Love for me was conditional. I was searching for love and validation in all the wrong places at the age of twenty-one. Honestly, I could have ended up in a much worse situation than my current marriage. My desperation for inclusion was leading me down a dark path that just ended in sex and broken hearts. I felt like Brad saved me. Like he pulled me from that crooked path and onto his straight, smooth course.

We were twenty-three when we got married. Young, but that age is pretty average for marriage in the Midwest. The idea of having kids was one we tossed around from time to time, never making a decision. Once I hit thirty and we still hadn't fallen in love with the idea of making a family, we officially decided kids weren't on the table for us. And that was fine. It meant more time for each other. At least that was what I told myself even after it became clear that the extra time was for golfing or video games or fantasy football.

It was clear early on that Brad wanted to marry his mother. She was a homemaker who took care of the kids, cooked all the meals, and cleaned the house. His dad never had to learn to be an active parent, nor did he have to provide anything for his family other than the money needed to keep the household afloat. And even though we didn't have kids, and even though I worked a full-time job, for some reason he still expected me to be the sole cook and housekeeper. And for years, I just handled everything. I knew that I chose this life, and it wasn't a bad life. Brad wasn't abusive, and he wasn't unfaithful. He was the general manager at our local grocery franchise, and he made decent money. And this life had set me up to be in a position at thirty-four years old to open my own clothing boutique. I can't complain.

And yet...

When I was working my last job, I started seeing a therapist to help find coping mechanisms for the stress I dealt with at work. It was bleeding into my life, and I was miserable all the time. But, of course, therapy addresses so much more than just what you go in for.

And my marriage became a huge topic of conversation. Gender roles, internalized misogyny, and emotional neglect were just a few terms used regularly. Between my therapist and Frankie pulling me out of my shell, I really started to figure out who I wanted to be. And I didn't want to be the timid wife who bent over backwards with little to no reward anymore. But I had established the status quo, and it was harder than I thought to wipe the slate clean.

Opening All Eras was a huge step to establishing my independence and showing Brad that I was capable of more. So much more. I had the potential to do anything I set my mind to, and I proved it with this business endeavor. I was proud of myself. Prouder than I ever thought possible. And he didn't seem to care.

My phone buzzes on the counter, pulling me from the trip down memory lane. An email pops up on my screen, reminding me that I have a delivery scheduled for today for some new jewelry I ordered for the store. I grab my stuff and head out the door.

***

About an hour after I opened the store, the bell over the door rings. I look up from my laptop on my front counter, expecting to see Kay or ladies in search of their next perfect outfit. Instead, a large man wearing a UPS uniform steps through the door. He's tall, over six feet. His hair is dark and shaggy, curling slightly at the ends that poke out under his hat. He has a dark goatee that is smattered in salt and pepper coloring. His short-sleeve shirt shows off the dark swirls of tattoos covering both arms. He catches sight of me and heads my way.

"Josephine Pearson?" His voice is deep and smooth. I can almost feel it glide over me like a piece of silk would glide over my skin.

Taken aback at the effect he seems to have on me, I blurt out, "Where's Kay?" His steps falter for a moment, and I realize that I must have come across as rude. "Umm, it's just that, um, they always deliver my packages." I smile sheepishly at him.

He makes it to my counter, setting the package down and handing me the signature pad. "Yeah, our routes got changed a bit, so you're stuck with me now." He smiles at me, and I notice deep dimples in both cheeks. When my eyes meet his, I notice the slight crinkles in the corners. This man has spent his life smiling and laughing. *What must that be like?* I catch myself looking at him longer than is socially acceptable and clear my throat as I look down to sign for the delivery.

"Well, I'm sad to hear that. They were a bright spot in my days anytime they brought me something." I hand back the signature pad.

"Now, come on, darlin'. I can be your bright spot! Kay is great, but they learned their charm from me." He winks at me, and I feel myself blush.

"I guess we'll see, won't we? If you can't live up to Kay, I might have to file a formal complaint." I smile slyly. *Am I flirting? What even is this?*

"Challenge accepted, Josephine," he says as he backs towards the door.

Right as he goes to step out, I say, "Call me Jo."

He looks back at me. "See you soon, Jo." The bell above the door dances with his departure, and I watch through the window at his tall, muscular frame as he climbs into his truck and heads off to the rest of his route. I release the breath that I didn't realize I was holding. *Well, shit. That man might be trouble.*

Later that night, as I'm getting ready for bed and trying to tune out Brad as he talks about preseason football, I realize that I never got the UPS driver's name.

***

Two days later, he's back. "Put your sunglasses on, Jo! Your bright spot has returned." He's smiling from ear to ear as he walks up to my counter. I can't help but laugh at his obnoxious charm as I pull the sunglasses that are still perched on my head down over my eyes. He throws his head back in a loud laugh. "Cute."

"I thought so," I reply as I sign for the package. "Hey, I never got your name." I look up to see him smiling down at me.

"Cole," he replies.

"Well, it's nice to officially meet you, Cole. I look forward to a beautiful friendship."

He leans forward and gently pushes my sunglasses further up my nose. His warmth envelops me, and I find myself leaning in slightly. "Me too, Jo. Me too," he replies softly. Then he's walking back toward the door. Before he steps outside, he turns back, smiling. "You just might be the new bright spot in my days, too." And then he's out the door.

Chapter 4

♥

"The idea you had of me, who was she?"

Fall blew in on the heels of August, the September air crisp. *This is my favorite time of year.* I inhale deeply, pulling the fresh air into my lungs as it blows in from the open kitchen window. My mind is wandering over the past few weeks: running the store every day, helping women find new outfits, and making connections, *Cole.* Cole. I haven't been able to get his crinkle-eyed smile out of my mind. I've seen him a few times since the store opened, and each time he seems thrilled to see me. And I would be lying if I said I wasn't thrilled to see him. He makes me smile in a shy way, like when you're a teenager with a crush. *Is that what this is? Do I have a crush?*

I shake myself of those thoughts as I hear Brad coming down the stairs. "Smells good, babe! Is everything going to be ready before the guys get here?" He struts into the kitchen, grabbing himself a beer from the refrigerator.

"Yeah, I'm almost finished here, and then I'll set it up on the table in the basement. Could you — "

He interrupts me as he starts to leave the kitchen. "Thanks, babe!" he hollers back, without even turning to look at me. *Guess I'll carry everything down myself.* Today is his fantasy football draft, and he volunteered to host without even asking me. And since we are hosting, it fell to me to make all of the food for it. I find the serving tray I bought a few years ago and start piling plates, utensils, and napkins on top of it.

A few trips later, all the food and serving dishes are in the basement, spread on the folding table Brad set up next to the TV. "Looks great, Jo." He grabs me by the waist and presses a hurried kiss to my cheek. The doorbell rings, and he heads off to start letting people in.

***

Listen, I love football just as much as the next person. But having to sit in this room listening to all these men discuss the stats of different players, defenses, kickers, yadda yadda yadda, is not how I want to be spending my evening. I got stuck entertaining the few wives that came with their husbands. I don't know these women, and it's made the last few hours super awkward. But they seem to be wrapping everything up.

"Dude, I still can't believe you changed up the draft order. Grabbing a QB in round two? What the fuck, man? You threw me off!"

"Sorry, man. Had to get Lamar before he was taken. He's not just the top-scoring QB, he's the top-scoring player, period!"

"Yeah, but you play me week one and I have the Vikings defense. Number one rushing defense in the league. We will see how Lamar fares against them."

I'm not even trying to pay attention to who is talking at this point. Instead, I am trying to politely herd everyone upstairs and out the door so that I can have my house back. I want to get out of these heels and into something comfortable; maybe read a book before bed. Having already decided to leave the dishes down here until tomorrow, I'm anxious to get to my self-care for the evening.

"Thanks for coming, guys! It's going to be a great season!" Brad yells out the front door at everyone as they get in their cars. I slip out of my heels as he closes and locks the front door. *Finally.* "Whew! What a night! I'm pretty stoked about my team!" Brad steps up in front of me, taking my heels out of my hand. "How about you and I head to bed, huh?" His tone drops suggestively. I should have seen this coming. He's had a little to drink. I should have known.

Knowing this probably won't take long, I lean in, hoping to still have some time for myself afterwards. I head towards the stairs leading up to the bedrooms, turning back with a sexy smirk when I get to the bottom. "Coming?" He quickly follows behind, smacking my ass as I start up the stairs ahead of him.

Once we're in the bedroom, he pulls off his shirt and strips off his pants. No preamble with this one. In just his boxers and socks, he gets on the bed, lying on his back with his hands behind his head. "Strip for me, baby," he says, attempting to be sexy.

Smiling, I untie the high-waisted sash and start unbuttoning the front of my dress. When enough buttons are loose, I let it fall to the ground, pooling at my bare feet. I unhook my bra and drop it on the floor with the dress. Finally, I slide my seamless plum panties down my legs and stand back up. Brad reaches for me, indicating that I should join him in bed.

I climb up next to him, sitting back on my heels. He sits up and takes my face in his hands, kissing me deeply. I can feel his tongue along the seam of my lips, trying to gain entrance. I let him in, tasting beer and the faint hint of mint. Our tongues tangle for a minute before he pulls away. "You get on top," he breathes as he lies back on the bed.

Pleasantly surprised at this choice of position, I pull his boxers all the way off, leaving him bare on our bed. Brad is an attractive man. I take in the sight of him, naked and erect. He's softer around the belly than he was when we met, but then again, so am I. But he takes care of himself, and the exercise he gets golfing shows in the lean lines of his torso. Straddling him, I hover over his cock, lining up with the folds of my pussy. I need a little friction before I attempt to work him inside. I glide back and forth, letting the tip of his cock hit my clit at just the right angle. He's of average size, and when he's willing to take direction, he knows how to use what he's been given.

Being on top is my favorite position, but it's not his preference. I'll take advantage of this as long as I can. My breathing picks up as he closes his eyes and moans. His hands find my hips, stilling me so he can angle his cock at my entrance. Slowly, he pushes up and in. Once I'm fully seated on him, I start to grind, letting my clit graze his pubic bone, feeling the orgasm start to build. But he sits forward, wrapping his arms around me and flips me over. Once we are settled with him on top, his thrusts grow rapid. He's pumping into me with no rhyme or rhythm as sweat builds on his forehead. I grab his back, just along for the ride, as he buries his face in my neck. I can hear his grunts and groans as he nears his climax. After a few more deep thrusts, he comes, letting his body weight fall on me as his heart rate slows.

Finally, he rolls off of me. He leans over to kiss me before getting up to go to the bathroom. I stay there, staring at the ceiling, waiting for him to be done so I can sneak the vibe out of my makeup bag and finish the job he rarely bothers to do anymore.

***

The dishes from the draft party sit on the table in the basement for the remainder of the weekend. When I realize he isn't going to clean up, I heave a heavy sigh and start bringing everything up to the kitchen. The television is too loud, blaring the analysts' projections for the upcoming football season, and I fist the trash bag in my hand as I tamp down the irritation of having to do this on my own. This is what I signed up for when I married Brad. And I thought that was fine. But I'm a different person than I was at twenty-three, and as I peer ahead into my future—ten, twenty, thirty years down the road—tears fill my eyes at the prospect that *this* is the rest of my life. *I don't think I can accept that.*

Chapter 5

♥

"I think it's strange that you think I'm funny, 'cause he never did."

Balancing the box precariously between my arm and my hip, I start to climb up the wobbly step ladder. I can just hear Frankie in my head. *I told you to wait until I could help you!* Well, if I don't fall, she won't know. I finally had a chance to reorganize the mess that is my office, and the last step was putting these storage boxes on the top of my wire shelving. Now on the top step of the ladder, I pull the box in front of me and start to lift it over my head to slide it onto the top shelf. At that moment, the bell over the front door rings, and the stepladder teeters over the groove in the tile floor. *No wonder it's wobbly. Next time I'll pay attention.* With the box over my head, my center of gravity is off, and I start to feel my balance go. "Oh, shit!" I shriek.

But then there's warmth at my back as a large hand is reaching over my head to grab the box, and the other tattooed arm slides around my waist to steady me on the ladder. I grab onto that arm for dear life while Cole slides the box onto the top shelf.

"Damn, darlin', you about gave me a heart attack," he says as he helps me down from the ladder. "Next time, wait until I'm here, and I can do this for you." *I swear to God, Frankie is laughing somewhere.*

"Sorry, I thought I had it, but I guess I didn't set the ladder right. Thank you for the assist. Won't happen again, promise." I realize he's still holding my waist as I go to mock salute my promise to him. My skin flushes, and I step backwards, away from the giant, beautiful man who may have just saved my life. *Is it hot in here? Jesus.*

"Well, I'm glad I got here in time to help," he replies as he walks out of the office and back around the front counter. "Wouldn't want you getting hurt." He bends down to grab the package he had left behind in pursuit of saving my life, and I can't help but admire the way his pants hug his ass and thighs. *This man never skips leg day.* My cheeks flush again as he turns, my eyes immediately darting to his face, hoping I wasn't caught. His eyes crinkle as he smiles down at me with a knowing gleam. *Yep, I was caught.*

"Thanks, again. Frankie would have my ass if I had injured myself when I could have just waited for her to be here to help. Glad I don't have to hear the 'I told you so' she would have given me without your help." I sign for the package, and he chuckles.

"Frankie's the loud one with the colorful tattoos that's always in here?"

"That's her. My loud, little menace!"

He laughs at my endearment. "Yeah, I wouldn't want to admit defeat to her either. Glad I could help." As he reaches the door, he turns with a bright smile and says, "See you soon, Sunshine." As always, the bell above the door is the soundtrack to his departure.

***

The next day, Cole comes in, wheeling a dolly with a giant box perched on it. "Sunshine! I got a big one for you today!" I run to the door to hold it open for him as he brings it in, preening a little on the inside from his use of *Sunshine* as a nickname.

"Ooooh, my new shelving unit for accessories!" I squeal with excitement. "This was supposed to get here before I opened, but it ended up on backorder. I couldn't find anything else I liked, so I decided to wait it out." I guide him over to the corner by the front counter where the box can sit, out of the way until I can get to it.

He slides the box off the dolly. "You got someone who can help you put it together?"

"I'm going to do it when the store closes. I put together everything else in here." I shrug, noting how his eyes dart to my wedding ring, and his brows furrow slightly. Ignoring the flutter this causes in my chest, I reach my hand out, waiting for him to hand me the signature pad.

He eyes me for a second longer before passing it over. He's unusually quiet as I sign and hand it back.

"Alright, Sunshine. Enjoy the rest of your day." He gives me his perfect, crinkly smile and heads out to the rest of his route.

***

At 7 o'clock on the dot, I flip the open sign off as I reply to Frankie's diatribe on the "Daddy kink" she didn't realize was in the new book she's reading. It's the one kink that makes her cringe. Age gap? She's good. Taboo? Loves it. But as soon as the FMC calls her man "Daddy," she's out; line drawn. *Make it make sense.* And in classic Frankie fashion, she can't DNF the book. Nope, she just bitches to me about it. I chuckle as I set the phone down and grab the scissors to cut open the box for the accessory shelf.

I flip my sound system from the Taylor playlist I had going to my current spicy audiobook. Deliciously filthy bedroom banter filters through the store's speakers on high volume as the bell over the door jingles, alerting me to the fact that I may have turned the open sign off, but I neglected to lock the door. *Fuck!* I scramble for my phone, trying to turn off the *not-suitable-for-work* dialogue currently blaring. "I'm so sorry!" I breathlessly yell toward the latecomer. But his booming laugh hits my ears before I face him, and I don't need to turn to know who I'll see.

"Interesting choice, Sunshine. Wouldn't have pegged you for a dark romance girly," Cole teases.

I swear, my entire body heats and turns red from embarrassment. "I wasn't expecting anyone to come in," I huff at him as I skirt around him to lock the door. "What are you doing here? And what do you know about dark romance?" I narrow my eyes slightly, letting him know I'm teasing.

"Figured I'd offer my help with the shelf. But it seems I interrupted something." He winks at me. "Pretty sure my sister just finished that particular book. Ruined cookies and cream ice cream for her, so of course, she had to ruin it for me. Thought it would be hilarious to whisper it to me as I was eating that exact flavor at my nephew's birthday party a few weeks ago."

I laugh out loud at the reference to the book I had, indeed, been listening to. "Your sister sounds delightfully evil."

"Delightfully is debatable. But evil, yes." He laughs as he looks around. "She'd love this store. And from what I've seen, you guys would probably get along."

"Loves dark rom-coms and would appreciate my eclectic taste? Yep, we'd get along," I laugh. "But seriously, you really don't have to do this. You must have better things to do after work than help me build a shelf."

"I really don't, Sunshine. Now, hand over the scissors." His smile is so warm, and he exudes confidence in a way that makes me believe him when he says he wants to be here. I hand him the scissors and watch as he cuts open the box. My body further heats as I watch him pull all the pieces out, his back muscles flexing under his shirt. My core starts to heat as my mouth waters, and I am flabbergasted by my reaction to this man. *This must be ovulation talking.*

He turns to start arranging all the pieces, and I startle, clearing my throat and jumping to move out of his way. "What can I do to help?"

"Not a thing, darlin'. You can go about your normal closing chores, and I'll work on this." His eyes meet mine, and I nod. "And feel free to put that audiobook back on. I might learn something." He gives me an exaggerated wink.

"Stop making fun of me," I chide. *My body cannot get any more red, right?*

"Wouldn't dream of it, darlin'."

I look pointedly at him as I turn the Taylor playlist back on, and he chuckles as his attention turns back to the shelf he's building.

***

We work in comfortable silence for about an hour, both of us wrapping up our respective jobs around the same time. I grab my purse as Cole piles all the trash into the cardboard box the shelf came in. It looks perfect, and it definitely took him much less time than it would have taken me. "Where do you want this, Sunshine?"

I show him the spot I had left empty for it, and he moves it over there with ease. "Thank you. I'm excited to come in early and rearrange some stuff. It's going to be fun to play with."

"Like a kid in a toy store," he says quietly.

"What?"

"Your eyes just lit up like a kid's in a toy store. You love this."

His attentiveness rattles me a little. He sees me, and I am not used to anyone being that observant. "I do. I really do." Looking up, I meet his deep hazel eyes. They're soft and shining, like my happiness means something to him. But that can't be. He doesn't even know me. After a beat too long, I pull my gaze away, saying shakily, "Should we head out?"

He smiles and grabs the box full of trash. "After you, darlin'." We walk out the door together, and he stands by while I lock up. He tosses the box in the dumpster as we pass it, but instead of walking to what I presume is his truck, seeing as it's the only other vehicle in the lot except mine, he follows me to my little SUV. I open the door and reach to set my purse on the passenger seat before straightening up and turning to him.

"Thank you for your help tonight. Truly."

"Anytime, Sunshine. Have a good night. Get home safe."

I slide into the driver's seat as he closes the door behind me. I start my car as I watch him walk over to the black pickup truck parked next to me. Effortlessly, he gets in, starting the loud engine. He looks my way, signaling me to leave first. As I pull out of the parking lot, I watch in my rearview mirror as he turns the opposite way to head wherever home is. And I suddenly feel desperate to know where that is...who he might be returning home to. Because even though I have someone waiting for me at home, the thought that he might have someone waiting for him as well stings.

♥

Chapter 6

I pull into the garage, noting that it's later than I usually get home, but not by much. Cole helping with the shelf was a game changer. When I enter the house, I see Brad sitting at the table, scrolling on his phone. He looks up when he hears me.

"Hey, Jo. A little late tonight." He sets his phone down, giving me his full attention.

"Yeah, I had that shelving unit come in. I stayed a little late to get it put together." I don't meet his eyes as I start setting my stuff on the counter, fiddling with something in my purse so I don't have to turn back to him. "I'm really not that late, though." I don't know how to begin to explain Cole's presence and his help at the store, so I opt to leave that information out. It's not a big deal anyway, right? He was just a good Samaritan, helping a local business owner. Right?

"I texted you. You couldn't have responded? Let me know you were going to be late?"

Shit. I wasn't paying attention to my phone at all while Cole was there. And it never even occurred to me that Brad would notice I was late. I finally stop fidgeting and turn to face him. "I was trying to get through everything so I could leave. I wasn't watching my phone."

He just looks at me for another moment, and I wish I knew what was going on in his head.

"So, what's for dinner?" he asks, as he picks his phone back up, letting me know he's done with this conversation.

I stare at him a moment, anger prickling at the edges of my senses. "I literally just walked in the door. I haven't even stepped all the way into the house, Brad."

He looks at me again, uncaring. "You're the one who cooks. It's not my fault you're home late." He resumes his scrolling.

The indifference in his tone amps up my anger. "You've been home for hours. You could have made something when you started getting hungry."

He scoffs. "Why would I make something when I thought you were going to be home to cook? Jesus, Jo, it's like you've forgotten how to be a wife when you're home."

My retort comes flying out before I have a chance to stop it. "Jesus, Brad, it's like you've forgotten how to be a grown-ass man." My posture goes rigid. *I can't believe I said that.* I brace myself for his reaction, never having spoken to him like that before.

Sardonic laughter leaves his lips as he stands from the table. "You know, you've never quite mastered the art of sarcasm, Jo. I'll order pizza," he says as he walks to the living room.

Are you fucking kidding me? I'm stone still as I try to figure how I feel about this entire interaction. For some reason a Mrs. Kim quote from an early season of Gilmore Girls flows through my head. *"Boys don't like funny girls."* I can't contain my laughter, and it bubbles out as I try to keep it quiet. *I'm losing it.* My husband is a complete ass, and my brain's response is to go completely empty with the exception of the most unhelpful show quote. *Fucking lovely.*

I finally get myself moving again, and I head upstairs. Since Brad is ordering pizza, I decide to take a bath while I wait for it to get here. I turn the faucet to my preferred temperature, letting it run while I get undressed. I pull my hair into a bun on top of my head and slide into the hot, inviting water. Tension seems to ease from my muscles as I relax and close my eyes. All I can think about is the stark difference between my evening at the store and my evening at home. More accurately, the stark difference between Cole and Brad. One man showed up, unprompted, just to help me. The other...well, the other did not. I ponder my feelings until I hear the doorbell and finally pull myself from the tub.

Once I'm dressed, I head downstairs, where Brad is sitting on the couch, eating his pizza in front of the television. The pizza box is sitting on the kitchen table. I open it to see a pizza piled high with Italian sausage; the one pizza topping that I absolutely do not like. A resigned sigh slips from my lips as I roll my eyes to the ceiling before turning to the refrigerator to begin pulling out the ingredients for a sandwich. *Message received, Brad.*

Chapter 7

♥

"And in a blink of a crinkling eye..."

October is the bane of my existence. A Midwest October means we bounce from temperature highs in the 80s to highs in the 30s every other day. My allergies are kicking my ass this morning, and I should be given some sort of award for crawling out of my warm bed to get ready for work.

Tuesdays are hit or miss for me at the store. I'm closed Sundays and Mondays, so I either get a rush of people who didn't make it before closing on Saturday, or I get nothing. Today has been a constant swell of people, which, normally, I love. But today, I've literally carried around a box of tissues as I help customers. I've gotten so tired of saying, "I promise, I'm not actually sick. It's allergies!" But I keep a healthy distance from everyone just to be considerate.

I hear my bell chime, and I see Cole enter out of the corner of my eye. I'm in the middle of a conversation with a customer that has the potential to be a gift basket that I get to build for her daughter. This would be an incredible opportunity to do something fun and creative while also showing off my skills to my other customers. Perfect social media post and a great gift for this young woman. I catch his eye and mime that he can sign for me. He nods and sets the package on my front counter. In my periphery, I see him sign his pad as a huge sneeze starts to force itself out of my nose. I throw a tissue to my face, hoping to muffle the obnoxious sound. As I apologize to my customer, I look to see Cole backing out the door. Our eyes meet, and he gives me his quintessential crinkle-eyed smile while I give him a little wave.

I turn back to the customer, eager to discuss the gift basket but also surprisingly sad that I didn't get my full ray of sunshine from Cole today.

***

A short time later, I'm behind the counter, ringing up a group of middle-aged women who are in their self-reported "Hot Mess Express" era. They've been hilarious, and I can't help thinking about Frankie. *That's going to be us someday.*

The bell over the door jingles, and I turn to greet the customer, but it's Cole. I'm surprised to see him. He's still in the middle of his route, and he's already been here today.

He walks up to the counter and sets an insulated cup out of the way of the women checking out. He leans in and quietly says, "Drink up, darlin'," before turning and heading out the door.

The interaction was so quick that the Hot Mess Express ladies didn't even notice him. *How could they not notice him?* We finish up their transaction, and I'm reaching for the cup before they're even out the door. I inhale a light, fresh scent from the hot beverage. Taking off the lid of the cup, I realize that he's brought me green tea. I take a sip, and it warms my whole body as it goes down. As I'm setting the cup down, I notice writing on the side.

Feel better, Sunshine. My days are cloudy when you're not shining.

I can feel my entire face light in a smile as happy tears fill my eyes. My toes curl from the pleasure I get from his words. His thoughtfulness astounds me. How is this man real? And why has he chosen to shine his light on me?

***

Saturday rolls around, and with it comes frigid winds. I'm hoping no storms come through, because right now, it would turn into snow. Despite the cold weather, people are out shopping, and the store has been busy today.

The time seems to fly by, and before I know it, I'm near closing. The store has just emptied out, and I am kind of hoping no one else comes in so I can wrap everything up for the weekend and go home at a decent time. I step into my office to take a sip of water when I hear the bell chime. I let out a quiet groan before fixing my face into a smile and turning to address the customer. But it's not a customer; it's Cole.

He's walking towards me holding a package in one hand. His UPS shirt is unbuttoned, showing a black Henley underneath. And good goddamn, he fills out that Henley *so* well. I've always read scenes in romance novels where the alpha male character is wearing the shit out of a Henley, but honestly, I didn't think Henleys existed in the real world. I've never seen a man wear one. But I must be around the wrong men because I have been missing out all my life.

"Hey, Sunshine," he says. His voice sounds tired.

"Hey, you're here late," I reply, taking the package from him.

"Yeah, this was supposed to be on my truck today, but it got left at the depot. I saw it when I got back and didn't want you to have to wait until Tuesday for it." He trails off, and I glance behind him, out the front window, to see his black pickup truck in the parking lot.

"You brought me this after you clocked out?" My surprise must show on my face because he furrows his brows a little as he meets my eyes.

"It might've been important. Didn't want you to go without." A slight blush creeps over his exposed cheeks. "It's no big deal, darlin'."

My eyes start to shine, and I can't believe I'm on the verge of tears right now. *Not a big deal??*

I sniff and blink my eyes to keep the tears at bay. "It's a very big deal," I whisper. "Thank you."

"Anything for my sunshine," he quietly replies, and I finally get the crinkle-eyed smile I've been missing.

"You look tired," I say.

"It's been a long week." He runs his hand through his hair, and I suddenly have a flash of his tattooed hand running through *my* hair, gripping it at the scalp, tugging my head where he wants it...

"You get a lot of business today?" His words startle me out of my fantasy, and I clear my throat, bringing myself back to reality.

"Yeah, it was actually pretty busy, considering the cold weather. But I'm ready for my days off." I smile up at him. "Though, I'm feeling much better after that green tea." I drop my eyes, too shy to meet his after saying that. But then I can't resist looking up at him from under my lashes. "Thank you for that. It was very sweet."

He leans closer to me over the counter. "I'm inclined to take care of you, Sunshine." His voice drops. "I want you to be able to keep shining."

My heart skips a beat in my chest. It feels so good to hear someone say they want to take care of me or that they care about my happiness and well-being. But my eyes catch on my wedding ring, and my heart plummets to my stomach. Why isn't my husband, the man who vowed to care for me, this considerate of me? He wasn't even this caring and thoughtful when we were dating, and the beginning of the relationship is when you're supposed to pull out all the stops.

Cole must notice a change in my temperament because he straightens up. "I better get home and let you close up."

Before he can leave, I reach across the counter and place my hand on top of his. His skin is warm, and that warmth seems to seep into my bones, creating a space in my heart that shouts "safety." *This man is good and safe.* "Thank you, Cole."

His eyes shift from our hands together to my face before he replies. "You're welcome, Jo." He slides his hand out from under mine, and then he's out the door.

Chapter 8

♥

"And if you wanted me, you really should've showed."

My plan to sleep in on Sunday is thwarted by Brad's shouts sounding from downstairs. Bleary-eyed, I look at my phone to see it's 8:30am. What could he possibly be shouting about so early?

I climb out of bed and throw on my robe, tying the belt around my waist as I step into a pair of slippers. I make my way downstairs, his shouts continuing to travel up two stories. Once I make it to the basement, I see him standing in front of the TV with a scowl on his face.

"What are you yelling about?"

Without even looking at me, he says, "My top-scoring wide receiver just got injured because someone doesn't know how to run a fucking route."

"Isn't it too early for football? It's not even 9 am," I say, confused.

Finally, he looks at me. "London game. Started at 8 am." Noticing my robe, he adds, "Sorry if I woke you." Then his attention turns back to the television.

Understanding that I've been dismissed, I head back upstairs to start my day.

***

Around 11:15, Brad ambles up the stairs. I've spent the last few hours cuddled on the couch in the main living room, reading my newest romance novel. He comes to sit beside me, and I slide my bookmark in between the pages before closing my book.

"That was a stressful game. But the noon games should be better," he says.

"Okay. So, you're going to spend the majority of the day down there?" I ask.

"Yeah, my entire team plays today, so I am going to use the multi-view to watch 4 games at once. Why? Did you need me for something?" He places his hand on my knee, rubbing gently.

Smiling, I respond, "No, I have nothing planned today."

He leans in to kiss my cheek. "Want to order something for lunch?" He must see the surprise on my face because he adds, "I'm sorry about the pizza the other night. That was petty. I don't want to make you cook today. You pick, and I'll order." He smiles at me like he's just offered me the world. But all I can focus on is his word choice...*I don't want to MAKE you cook today.* I'm a grown woman. He can't *make* me do anything. But he doesn't seem to understand that.

Deciding not to voice my irritation, I just nod. He stands up and kisses the top of my head. "Just let me know when you're ready for me to order." With that, he heads back downstairs.

I remain sitting, staring straight ahead. How do I address this? How do I start making changes in our marriage without Brad feeling blindsided? I don't know what to do, but I know I can't do *this*. I need a partner, someone who will be *with* me. I don't need someone who thinks I should blindly follow direction.

Knowing I won't find answers just sitting here, I grab my phone and set a reminder to make a therapy appointment tomorrow. Then I text Brad.

> If you call the Mexican place we like, I'll go pick it up. I want my normal order.

I set my phone on the couch, not waiting for his response while I go get ready to leave.

***

An hour later, I am sitting in front of the big-screen television, eating tacos out of a box on my lap while Brad hoots and hollers. The game switches to a commercial, and he turns to me as he takes a bite of his burrito.

"Oh shit, babe. I almost forgot to tell you that I need to switch cars with you tomorrow." He shovels another bite into his mouth. Since he's focused on his plate, I have time to school my reaction as instant frustration floods my body.

"And why is that?" I ask quietly.

Still paying more attention to his food than to me, he says, "I scheduled an oil change for my truck tomorrow since you're off work. I'll take your car to work so you can run my truck up there." Another forkful of cheesy burrito enters his mouth as anger warms me from my head to my toes. He didn't even run this by me before scheduling it. He just decided that my time isn't as worthy as his, and therefore, he can just fill it as he sees fit.

I wipe my mouth with a napkin before moving the box of food from my lap to the coffee table. Sitting up straight, I look at him but don't say anything. I will wait until he gives me his full attention. After another beat, he looks up at me, his mouth moving to chew the oversized bites he's shoving in.

"You don't think this is something you should have asked me about before just scheduling? I could have plans tomorrow." I speak calmly, but my rigid posture radiates angry intensity.

He finally swallows and sets his fork down. "There was nothing on the calendar, and the store is closed tomorrow. I thought it would be fine."

"That's not the point, Brad. You should have asked before presuming my time was free to fill with your errands. I don't schedule things for you on your days off. You should offer me the same courtesy."

"Babe, this is not a big deal. It won't even take that long." He sits back on the couch, opening his legs in the stereotypical manspread.

Trying my best to keep my cool, I respond, "If it won't take that long, why couldn't you schedule it for this Saturday, when you're off?"

"Babe, come on. This weekend is supposed to be nice, and it might be my last weekend to golf before winter sets in." His eyes dart from me to the television, where the game has resumed.

Understanding finally dawns on me. This is *his* life, and I am just living in it. I am a prop to be used as needed. Golfing and football come before my needs. I serve a role here, and it's not beloved partner. It's subservient wife. My appetite has disappeared, so I stand up without another word and head for the stairs.

"Babe, seriously— "

"There are trash bags in the end table. Clean this shit up before you come upstairs. I'll take your truck tomorrow." I cut him off and slam the basement door before I can hear his reply.

Chapter 9

♥

"Have I known you twenty seconds or twenty years?"

"**S**o, anyway, the main male character's name in this book is Sheldon. *Sheldon.* Can you believe that? It's like this author has never seen When Harry Met Sally." Frankie has hoisted herself up on my checkout counter and is sitting criss-cross applesauce, her black boots poking out from beneath her knees. She has a napkin spread open on her lap to catch the crumbs falling from the chocolate croissant she's currently tearing into bite-size pieces.

It's been almost a week since I stormed away from Brad, and it's been uncomfortable around the house. He's not sure what to make of me, and I'm not sure how much I want to push him right now. It's a lot of polite small talk and quiet nodding. I needed my best friend. I convinced her to work Saturday with me, but in exchange, we are going out for drinks after the store closes tonight. I'm not thrilled about the idea of going out, but she insisted I need the girl time. And she's right; I do.

"Um...I've never seen When Harry Met Sally..." I respond to her ramblings.

From the corner of my eye, I see her go stock-still as I keep sliding hangers into my newest shipment of shirts.

"I'm sorry...What did you just say? How have we been friends for five years and I am just now finding out about this travesty?" She pops the last bite of croissant into her mouth, balls the napkin in her fist, and hops off the counter. She tosses the napkin in the trash, giving herself a moment to chew and swallow before leaning into my personal space. "This must be rectified immediately. It's only one of the best movies ever made!"

I start laughing as she stomps to the other side of the store, straightening items on tables. She throws her hands in the air, yelling, "This is not funny, Josephine!" *Oh shit, she full-named me.* "You do not understand how hard it is to imagine a sexy Sheldon while Billy Crystal's voice is in my head saying, 'Do it to me, Sheldon. You're an animal, Sheldon. Ride me big, Sheldon.'" She draws out both syllables in the last "Sheldon," and I double over in laughter.

"Okay, you're right. I need to watch this movie." I catch my breath as my laughter eases.

"I know you do. I'm tempted to cancel our drinks tonight and watch that movie instead, but I really need to go out." Frankie is married with a kid, and while she adores her family, sometimes she needs to be able to spread her wings a little. Drinks tonight is killing two birds with one stone. She needs it just as much as I do.

"Oh shoot, I forgot to mention to Brad that we are going out." I scurry to my purse and pull out my phone, shooting him a text with my plan for this evening. He's not going to like it, but I really don't care. Tossing my phone back in my purse, I notice it's two minutes until the store opens.

I'm unlocking the door as Frankie replies, "Fuck him. You're having fun tonight."

***

The day passes quickly. With Thanksgiving looming, people are officially starting their Christmas shopping, and luckily, that brings a lot of people into my store. Frankie and I alternate between working the front counter and straightening up messes left by hurried customers.

By the time I'm turning off the open sign, I realize I didn't see Cole today. I've gotten used to seeing him a couple times a week, and I find myself missing him on the days I don't see him. It feels like I've known him longer than just a few months. Our connection doesn't really make sense, considering we only see each other for a few minutes at a time, every few days. But there's something magnetic about him that pulls me to him. And when he's nearby, I want to sink into his warmth like a steamy bath. I'm picking up that he feels similarly, but neither of us knows what to do with this chemistry. I mean, I'm a married woman, after all. And I don't even know what his personal life looks like.

I'm jolted from thoughts of Cole as Frankie starts grabbing her things. She pulls on her coat and throws her purse strap over her shoulder. "Okay, I'm going home to change. Are you going to be here much longer?"

"Nope, I'm just going to count the drawer, and then I'm out," I say as I start pulling cash out of the drawer.

"I'll text you when I am on my way to your house." Her back is leaned against the door, ready to push back and leave. "Don't let asshat give you a hard time about going out. You deserve to have fun every once in a while." She gives me a pointed look.

"I know, babe." I sigh. "It'll be fine. See you soon." I wave her out and lock the door behind her. My eyes wander over the empty parking lot as I wonder why I feel sad when I don't see a familiar black pickup truck.

Chapter 10

♥

"And by the way, I'm going out tonight."

Grabbing my stuff, I hurry out of the car and into the house to see Brad leaning against the kitchen sink, waiting for me.

"Hey," I say. "I don't mean to rush by you, but I have to get changed before Frankie heads over." I start to hustle out of the kitchen when Brad grabs my elbow, stopping me in my tracks.

"Did you not get my text?"

I hadn't looked at my phone since texting him this morning. I didn't want to deal with this exact response. I roll my eyes as I say, "No, Brad. Even with Frankie there to help, I was slammed all day."

He lets go of my elbow, but I remain standing in the middle of the kitchen, waiting for him to speak. "Do you really think it's a good idea to go out tonight when it's been so off between us lately?"

That gives me pause. What does he think is happening here? "What do you mean, Brad? What does one thing have to do with the other?"

"Well, it seems odd that we are having issues, and this is when you choose to go out partying with your friend." He crosses his arms over his chest, like he's caught me in something.

"We are having issues because you don't respect me as a person, Brad. Everything I am and everything I do is in relation to you somehow. You don't actually see me as an equal in this relationship. And regardless of what is happening between you and me, I am entitled to my own personal time. If I want to use that time to—what is the word you used—party." My fingers mime air quotes as I say it. "With my best friend, then that's exactly what I'll do." I huff out a breath as my arms fall to my sides.

"That's bullshit, Josephine. I respect you. But I also don't want my wife gallivanting all over town while her best friend encourages her to make poor choices."

I start laughing. I can't help it. Does he not hear himself?

"You're laughing? This is not funny, Josephine."

Catching my breath, I say, "You keep saying my full name, like I am your child and you're trying to let me know this is serious. Do not speak to me like I am a child, Bradley," I emphasize the last syllable in his full name. "What is it you think Frankie and I are going to do tonight, huh? Why are you so worried?" Now it's my turn to cross my arms over my chest. I don't know what has gotten into me, but I refuse to stand down this time.

"She doesn't like me, Jo." He throws his hands in the air. "She never has. And yet you still choose to be friends with her!"

"So now I can't be friends with someone just because they don't like you? That's asinine, Brad. She's been there for me in ways no one else has. Maybe you should make a better effort with her and be happy your wife has such a supportive person in her life!" I am yelling now, and I don't know how to come down from this. "I am going out tonight. Frankie and I are going to have a few drinks, talk about life, and then come home. Not a big deal!" I turn and start making my way upstairs. Brad is hot on my heels.

"So you're just going to sit around and bitch about me? About our issues? And you think that's going to help us right now, Jo?"

I turn swiftly, causing him to step down. "Yes, Brad. Venting my frustrations allows me to clear my head a little and helps me figure out how to deal with the issues at hand. Maybe, getting it all out tonight with Frankie will make me like you more when I get home tonight." I turn back around, getting to the top of the stairs and heading into our bedroom.

Brad follows me and settles on the edge of the bed as I enter our closet and start grabbing clothes. Quietly, I hear him say, "Will you be interested in having sex tonight? Because it's sure been a while."

I freeze. Is he serious?

I march back into the bedroom. "You just spent the last five minutes talking about how things have been off between us and how we have stuff to deal with. And you're surprised I haven't been interested in being intimate with you?" I am utterly baffled right now. "The last few weeks have made me realize how little you value me and my contributions, so forgive me if that doesn't cause me to jump into bed with you. Jesus, Brad. For a smart man, you can be really dumb." I head back into the bathroom, stripping off my shirt as I go.

"I'm sorry, okay?" he calls through the doorway. "I didn't mean to make you feel undervalued. I value you! I love you! I don't know what you want from me."

I strip out of the remainder of my clothes and find the black lace bodysuit I bought a while back. I pull it on and then tug on a pair of tight, black jeans over it. Brad has made his way into the bathroom and is standing in the doorway, staring at me. I shrug on a cream-colored cropped cardigan and pull on some socks and my tall black boots. Pushing past him, I pull my hair out of its clip, fluffing it with some hair spray as it settles in messy waves around my face.

"You're not going out like that."

I catch sight of Brad in the mirror, and his eyes travel down to my ass and then up to my breasts in the mirror. Dabbing on some lip gloss, I make eye contact with him in the mirror. "You don't get a say in how I dress. Plus, there is nothing wrong with this outfit."

"You look too good to go out like that without me."

I scoff at him. "You can't be serious."

"Jo," he pleads.

"Brad, how little do you think of me? You think that just because we are having issues, I am going to go out and pick up a man? If you believe that, we have bigger issues than I realized." I shake my head as I slip around him to grab my little, black clutch. My phone buzzes as I am switching items from my purse into the clutch. "Frankie is here."

I walk to where he still stands in the bathroom doorway. Leaning in, I kiss his cheek. "I won't be out late. I'll see you when I get home."

Leaving him standing in our bedroom, I head out the door and slide into Frankie's passenger seat.

Chapter 11

♥

"You and I ended up in the same room at the same time."

Frankie lets me stew in silence for the entire car ride to the bar. She picked a lively place with a dance floor and a live band. Once we find a tall two-seater table and get settled in, she finally speaks, "How bad was it?"

"Bad. And I wasn't any better. I said some things out of anger. I could have handled it better. I *should* have handled it better." My head drops into my hands, my elbows perched on the tabletop. My hands scrape down my face as I lift to look at her. "I don't know what to do anymore. It's like I've outgrown him. How do I make someone grow to meet me where I am? I can't go back, Frankie. I can't be less than I am."

"Oh, babe." She grabs the edge of my chair, pulling me closer to her, and wraps me in her arms. "You should never be less than you are. But I don't have the answers for you. You have to figure this out with Brad."

I pull out of her embrace, nodding, as the waitress makes her way to our table. We order our drinks and a couple appetizers. As the waitress leaves to put our order in, I straighten my spine and look at Frankie. "I don't want to talk about Brad tonight. I just want to enjoy myself."

"I think that's an excellent idea," she replies.

***

Before we know it, we've polished off the appetizers we ordered and finished two rounds of drinks. The band has picked up in volume, and the dance floor is filling up. Frankie grabs my hand, tugging me to the middle of the floor. I laugh as we start dancing, our bodies moving to the beat of the music. I let myself move freely, bouncing and swaying, flowing with the wave of people around us.

After a few songs, Frankie leans in, placing her mouth by my ear so I can hear her. "There's a dude at the bar checking you out." She pulls away and winks at me, nodding her head behind me. I turn, my eyes wandering over the bar patrons before landing on a familiar pair of crinkly brown eyes. Cole. He smiles, and I can feel my entire face light up. I grab Frankie and start heading his way. "Let's go say hi!" I take the time to admire his form as we head over to the bar. He's wearing a pair of worn-blue jeans that hug his thighs in all the right places. The black Henley is back, unbuttoned at the collar. His sleeves are pushed up to his forearms, showing off the black swirls of tattoos crawling from his wrists up his arms and drawing attention to his large, callused hands. *Oh, what those hands would feel like roaming my body.* I shock myself with the direction my thoughts have taken and look back at Frankie to clear my head.

As I get closer, Cole turns sideways so I have room to sidle up to the bar with him. He leans down and greets me with, "Sunshine."

"Hi," I say with a shy smile.

Frankie stands next to me, leaning into my shoulder. "Delivery man," she says in greeting.

He chuckles. "Menace," he says in response.

She laughs out loud as she turns to me. "Did you tell him to call me that?"

I shake my head. "He must have figured out you're a menace all on his own." I laugh as my eyes meet his.

"Frankie, you're easily spotted as trouble from a mile away," he grins at her.

"Fair enough," she says with a smile.

Turning back to me, Cole asks, "Can I buy you ladies a round?" I nod, and he calls the bartender over to take our order. While we wait for our drinks, Cole smiles at us again. "You ladies looked good out there." His eyes land on me. "You looked free. Happy." He lifts his beer bottle to his lips, taking a quick swig. His eyes never leave mine, but my eyes trail his lips over that glass bottle. His tongue peeks out to lick a drop of beer off the rim. I feel my face flush, and I have to squeeze my thighs together as I imagine those lips and that tongue wandering over the hidden places on my body. My eyes travel back up to his, and I see nothing but heat and desire flash in them.

The moment is broken by the bartender, sliding my drink across the bar to me and handing Frankie hers. We sip in silence for a moment before Frankie finally says, "Well, are we going back out there?" She looks from me to Cole, then back to me. There's a glint in her eyes, and I know she knows what's going on in my head. She's letting me take the lead, taking her cues from me. But I also know she wouldn't let me make a decision I couldn't come back from.

Cole sets his now empty bottle on the bar. "You ladies have fun. I'm about to take off, but I'm glad I got to see you." He signals to the bartender as he pulls his wallet out of his back pocket. Pulling a few bills out, he hands them over, letting the guy know he can keep the change. "Keep an eye on your drinks, and be safe, okay?"

He nods to Frankie and then leans down to whisper in my ear, "Shine bright, darlin'." His breath is warm on my neck, and I shiver from the sensation. I almost whimper as he pulls away, not ready to relinquish the feelings he elicits in me anytime he's near. But as Cole steps back, Frankie grabs my left hand, hitting my wedding ring as she positions her hand in mine. And I'm reminded of Brad's worries about tonight. Guilt floods my system. Cole seems to see it happen, because he steps even further away, nodding at us before he turns and walks toward the exit.

Chapter 12

♥

"I had a marvelous time ruining everything."

Brad was waiting up for me when I got home later that night. We were both silent as we got undressed, brushed our teeth, and climbed into bed. I lay awake long after Brad's snores began reverberating through the room. I was at a loss. I couldn't look at Brad without instantly feeling angry lately. Once I opened my eyes to how he really seemed to view me, I couldn't stop seeing it. And it wasn't okay. I also seemed to be attracted to another man. Would I be feeling this way toward Cole if I wasn't so unhappy with Brad? I tossed and turned as my swirling thoughts held me in a vice grip. I finally fell into a fitful sleep, while dreams of Stepford wives haunted me.

***

Thanksgiving festivities put a pause on the issues Brad and I were having. His parents always hosted a dinner at their house, and then we always hosted a dinner with his friends. He and I found a way to come together to get through both events. To everyone around us, we were normal. Happy and content, Brad and Jo. But icy hostility coated the air when it was just the two of us.

He wanted things to go back to the way they were before I opened the store. But did he realize how isolating that was? Before I opened the store, I felt like I had very little meaning in life. He and Frankie were the only things that brought me joy. I had nothing for myself. Was that what he wanted? For me to be entirely reliant on him for validation? How could anyone sustain that? And why would you want that for someone you claimed to love? I wanted growth, together. Or I thought I did. The more therapy sessions I had, the more I realized I wasn't sure if I wanted to put forth the effort it would take to grow together. Plus, if I'm being honest, I didn't think Brad was capable of the change I wanted. And is it fair to expect him to change everything just because I ended up being different than what he wanted? Any serious conversations we attempted were just cyclical, spiraling back to the fact that he didn't understand me anymore, and I couldn't see how he didn't.

My mind was a helpless place to be in most of the time. It was like a vortex of negative emotion, threatening to swallow me whole. The only reprieve I got was when I was working at the store. The closer we got to Christmas, the busier I became. Even my moments with Cole were brief, though he was coming in more often due to my constant need to restock items. Despite how short the moments were, they always left me feeling lighter. His smile and the air around him always lifted my soul out of the hole it was in, setting it back within the sun's reach. Our brief encounters were recharging my batteries, and I couldn't figure out how that made me feel. And at night, it added one more plaguing thought to the vortex.

***

A week before Christmas, I find myself sitting at the kitchen table, staring out the window at the swirling snow. The clink of silverware being set on a plate brings my attention back to Brad.

"Sorry, did you say something?" I ask as I pick up my fork and start scooting food around my plate.

He just stares at me a moment before sighing and saying, "Did you call my grandmother to see what we need to bring to Christmas dinner this year?"

I set my fork down. Why is this my job? It's *his* grandmother. "No, I didn't. She's your grandmother; I figured you could call her."

"But you always call her," he responds.

I let out a frustrated sigh. "I shouldn't have to, Brad." I toss my napkin onto my plate. "Plus, I can't go this year. She planned it for the Saturday afternoon before Christmas. I have to work. I can't close the store on the last good shopping day before Christmas." Standing, I grab my plate and head to the sink.

He leans back in his chair, watching me as I turn the water on and begin rinsing dishes. "See, this is why you shouldn't have opened your own store." I hear his fork scrape across the plate as his napkin is harshly tossed on top.

I set down the dishes in my hand, placing my palms flat on the bottom of the sink as I close my eyes and take deep breaths. The water keeps flowing over my fingers, but I barely feel it. Brad can't seem to read the room because he just keeps talking. "You should never have started something that could impact your ability to be with family. I'm starting to believe the store is the reason for all our problems, Jo."

His voice sounds like it's far away as my vision starts to tunnel. I keep taking deep breaths, trying to stay calm. When my vision opens back up and my hearing returns to normal, I lift my hands out of the sink, turn off the faucet, and grab the hand towel. I gently dry my hands as I slowly turn to face Brad. He's sitting there, smugly, expectantly. And it's that moment when I know what I need to do.

I set the hand towel back on the counter and slowly walk over to Brad. He sits up in his seat, and I take a deep breath before strongly stating, "I want a divorce."

Part 2

January

"Relationships are like traffic lights. And I just have this theory that I can only exist in a relationship if it's a green light."
-Taylor Swift

Chapter 13

♥

"It was the end of a decade but the start of an age."

Josephine

"You really do have the best view."

"I know, right?"

The fireworks explode high above the empty field behind Frankie's house. We sit together, huddled in blankets on her deck, ringing in the new year. A cold breeze clashes with the hot air coming from her outdoor heater, and I take a sip of my Irish coffee. *Decaf, because, well, it's midnight.*

She turns her head toward me, laying her cheek against her knees, which are pulled up close to her chest. "Any resolutions this year?"

I take another sip of my drink, savoring the warmth of the mug against my chilled hands. "I don't think I want to make any resolutions this year. I just want to make decisions for myself and keep moving forward."

She scoots closer to me on the patio sofa and lays her head on my shoulder. Following suit, I rest my head against hers. "This is going to be a great year for you, Jo. And just the beginning of an entirely new life," she whispers.

We sit in silence a moment longer before we hear her back door slide open. Turning, we see Parker stick his head outside. Meeting Frankie's eyes, he smiles and says, "Come here, babe."

Chuckling, she unwinds herself from her blanket and hurries over to her husband, where they share a brief kiss. "Happy New Year," he whispers.

"Happy New Year." She smiles against his lips as she kisses him one more time.

"Alright, ladies, seriously. Come inside now. It's too damn cold out here." He steps back inside but waits to make sure we are following. After we've made it inside and closed the door, he wishes us goodnight and heads to bed.

I start to make my way to their guest room when Frankie speaks. "Dude."

I turn back to her, eyebrows raised, waiting for her to finish her thought.

"I love you."

"I love you, too."

***

Sleep evades me, and I watch the slowly rotating blades on the ceiling fan above my bed. I've been at Frankie's since the night I told Brad I want a divorce. Two weeks. Two weeks in this weird limbo.

He was shocked when I dropped that bomb on him, and I took that opportunity to run upstairs and start packing a bag. I knew I had to get out of there before he started any kind of dialogue. When I came downstairs, he was still sitting at the kitchen table. He was staring at his hands, but when he heard me approach, he turned, jumping up from his seat when he saw me with a bag. He was desperate to get me to stay. He tried everything, cycling from apologizing to condescension to anger, back to apologizing. But I stood my ground. I stayed calm and just kept reiterating that neither of us were happy. Neither of us needed to live this way.

I finally got out of there after he somehow convinced himself I just needed a night to cool down. I called Frankie before I was even out of the driveway. She talked to me all the way to her house, and I managed to keep it together until I got there and saw her waiting on her front porch for me. I immediately broke down. Frankie had to help me out of the still running car. Before grabbing my bag, she had slid into the driver's seat to shut off the car and then led me into her house, depositing me in her guest room. She just tucked me right into bed and let me cry.

Once I calmed down, she sat there with me as I told her what happened. We talked through all the options. Did I want to go back? Did I want to try to work it out? Did I think couples therapy was worth a try? And every time I thought about an option that led *back* to my life with Brad, I broke down all over again. My marriage was over. I didn't know what was coming next, but that much I knew.

The first week, he called every day. I refused to see him, but I took every single one of his calls. And again, they ranged in emotion. He apologized; he told me I was overreacting; he got angry; he called me selfish. And all the while, I sat and listened. I never raised my voice. I never interrupted him. There was no point. I let him get it all out. And at the end of each call, I made sure he knew that my decision hadn't changed.

Luckily, he never showed up unannounced at Frankie's. But he did keep pushing me to meet him somewhere. After I was adamant that I would not come back to the house while he was there, he tried to meet for coffee, for dinner, for breakfast. I always declined. He also had the decency to refrain from showing up at the store. I continued working; my anxiety peaked each day, wondering if he was going to show up. But he never did.

Christmas was sad. Frankie included me in all of her festivities since I didn't have family to see. But I was still lonely and a little broken. Brad called on Christmas, and it was our first amicable discussion about the state of our marriage. I could tell he was worn out. He was sad. But he was starting to hear me, to understand I was unwavering in my decision.

The second week, the calls weren't daily anymore, but we texted every day. I went back to the house to get more of my clothes and essentials. But still, it felt like a weird limbo. Purgatory for separated couples.

The fan blades continue rotating as I force my mind to change direction, to stop focusing on what has happened and start looking forward. It's a new year. I'm separated from my husband. I'm living in my best friend's guest room. And I need to figure out next steps. I sit up in bed, turning on the light. I pull the journal off the bedside table and open it to a blank page. I start making a list:

Hire divorce attorney.

Get my stuff out of the house.

Find a new place to live.

Only three steps. Only three action items, but actually doing them seems insurmountable. But this is a new year, and I am determined to put myself first. And carrying the baggage from my past into my future is not on my list. Determination overcomes my melancholy, and I close the journal, sliding it back on the bedside table. I turn out the light and close my eyes. As I begin to fall asleep, one thought rings through my head: *I will not stand in my own way.*

Chapter 14

♥

"I pretend you're mine all the damn time."

Cole

Today marks the fifth day that she hasn't worn her wedding ring. I don't mean to keep track, but I can't help it. Right before Christmas, Jo seemed to deflate. I saw her twice before she closed for the holiday, and both times she seemed to be withering away in front of me. Dark circles marked her tired eyes, which no longer held the feisty glint I came to yearn for. My ray of sunshine had been replaced by a storm cloud.

Then, once she reopened after Christmas, I saw the empty spot on that important ring finger. I tried not to overthink it. It was just Christmas. Maybe her husband bought her a new ring, and it needed to be resized. Maybe they took her old one in to be cleaned.

But I've been in the store every day, not just dropping off packages but picking up items to be shipped. Apparently, Jo's new online shopping feature is getting as much attention as the storefront is. And every day, I can't help but notice that empty finger.

She was closed yesterday for New Year's Day, and I was thrilled to see her name on my list when I got into the depot this morning. I spent New Year's Eve with my sister and my nephew. We made sparkling punch with maraschino cherries and let him stay up until midnight to watch the ball drop. As I watched my sister hug her son and dance along to the sounds of the fireworks outside, I found my thoughts drifting to Jo. With that absent wedding ring, was it possible her husband wasn't kissing her at midnight this year? Then I envisioned her, a year from now, in my arms as I pull her in for a midnight kiss. My chest had tightened at the fantasy, and I had to shake myself out of that hopeful place. I knew nothing about this woman other than how she made me feel every time I saw her. But I hadn't earned that strange sense of hope.

I bring myself back to the present as she wraps up a transaction with a customer.

"Receipt is in the bag," she says as she hands the bag across the counter. "Happy New Year!" Her tone is chipper, and there is a smile on her face. But she's good at faking it with the customers. I need to see if that positivity lingers when she sees me. I don't want to see those slight shoulders droop anymore.

I step out of the way as the customer heads toward the front door, and Jo finally turns to me. Her smile relaxes into something more genuine, and I feel my face lighting up in return.

"Happy New Year, Sunshine." I set her package on the front counter and hand her the signature pad. My eyes, once again, dart to the empty ring finger on her left hand.

"Happy New Year, Cole." She scribbles her name and hands the pad back to me. But I am not ready to leave.

"Did you do anything special to ring in the New Year?" I ask, trying not to sound like I'm fishing for information.

"Frankie and I stayed up until midnight so we could watch the fireworks. Her house backs up to the field where they shoot them off, so we had the best view."

So she was with Frankie. Was her husband there? Did she go home to her husband? Why was I desperate to learn more details? "Girls night, huh? Sounds like a great way to ring in the new year. I hope you were safe driving home." Yeah, no one ever said subtlety was my strong point.

"Oh...yeah..." She hesitates a moment but then continues, "I've been staying with Frankie the last couple of weeks." She drops her gaze to the counter and lowers her voice before she adds, "My husband and I separated before Christmas, so it was an interesting holiday season this year." She finally looks back up at me, wariness in her expression.

I reach across the counter and gently grab her hand. "I'm sorry to hear that, darlin'." *Lies.*

Her hand tightens around mine. "Thanks, Cole. But it's for the best. It's time for me to start living my life for me, you know?" She blows out a breath and straightens her spine, her eyes meeting mine, determination shining in them.

Unearned pride swells in my chest. I have no right to feel this way, but I'm just glad this woman was able to choose herself. "I do. You deserve to live a life that serves you, Jo. A life that lets you shine." I smile at her, squeezing her hand one more time before letting go. Reluctantly, I turn to head out the door. As much as I would like to skip the rest of my route and convince this beautiful woman to take a chance on me, it's too soon, and I need to keep my job.

Before I begin pushing open the door, her voice pulls me back.

"Cole."

Turning around, I see her coming out from behind the counter. "Yeah, darlin'?"

She looks nervous. Her eyes dart around the store for a moment, and she anxiously wrings her hands. But then I see that determination sink back in, and she meets my eyes again. "Would you want to get coffee or something? Get to know each other away from the store?"

I swear, my heart stops beating in my chest for a fraction of a second. Is this really happening? How did I get this lucky? Not wanting to make her wait, I quickly answer, "I would love that, Sunshine."

"Great." She turns on her heel, reaching across the counter for one of her business cards and a pen. She scribbles something on it and then marches over to me. Yes, marches. That determination is really something. I hold in a chuckle, not wanting her to misinterpret my amusement. She hands me the card. "That's my cell phone number."

Gingerly, I take the card from her outstretched hand. I know this must be a big step for her, and she's probably feeling vulnerable, so instead of pocketing the card, I tuck my signature pad under one arm and pull my cell phone out of my pocket. I pull up my texts, create a new one, and type in her number.

We hear a faint chime come from the direction of her office, and she turns her head slightly. "Now you have mine. I'll text you when I get done with my route, okay?"

She nods and watches me as I repocket my phone and push open the front door. I can't help the smile that overtakes my face as I walk back to my truck. *What a year this is already turning out to be.*

Chapter 15

♥

"'Cause I see sparks fly whenever you smile."

Josephine

What the fuck?! Did I really just do that??

I'm still standing in the same spot as I watch Cole drive away in his giant truck. *I cannot believe I just asked a man out!* I'm panicking. I'm also experiencing the best butterflies in my stomach. But I'm panicking.

I finally manage to uproot myself and run back to my office, frantically grabbing for my phone. There's a text from an unknown number.

Talk soon, Sunshine. Enjoy the rest of your day.

I save the number and then open my contact list, scrolling until I find Frankie's name. I hit the call button, switch it to speakerphone, and impatiently wait for her to answer.

"Who died? What's wrong?" No hello, no greeting. But we never call each other, so that tracks.

"No one died. But I did just ask a man on a date."

Silence. Remember what I said about my loudest friend being silent? It's never good, and I cannot handle it right now.

"Frankie! I asked a man on a date, and I am freaking out! Speak!" I start pacing back and forth in my tiny office.

"Dude, sorry. I'm trying to process. Who did you ask?"

"Cole." I pause my pacing, anxious to hear her reaction.

"Oh my god, yes! He's hot, babe! Did he say yes?"

"Yes. I wrote my number down and gave it to him, and he texted me right then."

"This is great, Jo! Why are you freaking out?"

"Frankie, seriously? Where do I even begin?" My pacing begins again. "First, I literally just left my husband. We haven't even started any official process for separation or divorce. Second, I haven't been on a first date since college, so I have no idea how to date as an actual adult. What will people say?" I halt in my tracks, my heart rate increasing, which is actually concerning, considering it was high before. "Oh my god, Frankie. People are going to think I cheated on Brad!" I set my phone on the desk and dig the heels of my hands into my eyes. I can't do this.

"Jo, take a breath. This is just a date. Moving on after a marriage or relationship ends is a lot like grief. No one really knows what that process looks like until you're in it, and it's different for everyone. There is no timeline for how you move on. Yes, you just left Brad, and you still have a lot to figure out. But that doesn't mean you can't have some fun with other people while you're figuring stuff out. You're not jumping into another marriage; you're going on one date. One. That's all it has to be."

She pauses while I scrape my hands down my face, staring at the ceiling like there might be answers there.

"Are you okay?" Her voice is quiet through the phone.

"Yeah. Yeah, I think I'm okay. I was just not expecting this. And the fact that I am the one that initiated it is like...an out-of-body experience. I don't even know what I was thinking." I sit down in my chair, pulling the phone across the desk to me.

"Well, it sounds like you were thinking with your vagina. Cole's hot, babe! And it's been a while since you've had really satisfying sex. Let this man take you out, and hopefully, you can get some yummy orgasms out of it."

I laugh as I hear the bell chime out front. *Damn, I am so lucky no one witnessed that meltdown.* "Someone just walked in, so I have to go. But thank you for letting me freak out all over you."

"Anytime. You know that. Keep me posted! I'll want details!"

I hang up, sliding my phone in my back pocket as I step out to greet the new customer. While the woman browses, I think about what a huge step I took today. Was it wise to ask someone out mere weeks after leaving my husband? Maybe not. But I felt compelled to do it, and I acted on it. That's growth, and I need to be proud of it. It's scary as shit, but I did something that I wanted to do just because I wanted to do it. It's going to keep being scary until I get used to allowing myself this freedom. I pull my phone out of my pocket and open the text app, pulling up Cole's message.

> Thank you, Cole. Can't wait to talk later :)

I smile, allowing myself to feel those butterflies in my stomach again. I drift through the next few hours, his crinkle-eyed smile living rent-free in my head.

***

It's almost closing time when the door above the bell rings, signaling another customer. Now that I don't have to worry about getting dinner on the table for Brad, staying at the store later is not a big deal. I smile at the thin, blonde woman who walks in. She wears a dark camel-colored belted wrap coat, tight blue jeans, and light brown booties. I have to refrain from calling her Serena Van der Woodsen, but the Gossip Girl character has nothing on this woman.

"Welcome to All Eras," I call to her.

She smiles as she heads toward the counter. "I'm sorry I'm coming in so close to closing time. I've been wanting to get in here since you opened, but my schedule is crazy, and I have a kiddo, and," she cuts herself off to let out a tired laugh. "Well, things are just crazy in my world." She looks around, admiring the store.

"I totally understand. My world is a little upside down right now," I laugh. "No worries at all. Stay as long as you like."

"Thank you." She smiles again before continuing on to peruse items throughout the store.

As she shuffles through some blouses hanging on a rack near me, I ask her, "Is there anything specific you're looking for?"

"Oh, no, I never know what I want," she chuckles. "I'm a nurse, so I spend so much of my time wearing scrubs. Whenever I decide to dress in normal clothes, I always want to change it up. But then I never know what to look for or what's trending." She stops her searching and turns to me. "Anything you recommend?"

The idea that this fashionable woman doesn't know what's trending is absurd. "Honestly, you look incredible in what you're wearing. I would have never known you struggle to put outfits together."

She laughs again as she gestures at her coat. "This is tried and true. I stick with what I know."

"Well, it works for you. But anything in here would flatter you. If you find something you like, you can always try it on."

She makes her way around the store, and we continue small talk. Despite our initial interaction being so open, I can tell she's timid. But our conversation flows easily until she's carrying a handful of items up to the checkout counter.

"This has been exactly what I needed today," she says as she reaches into her purse for her wallet. "Thank you for letting me shop even as you were about to close. I didn't realize how much I needed to get out and do something for myself." Her eyes meet mine, and I pause at her last statement.

"I'm learning that self-care is very important. I'm so glad my store could be that for you today." I continue ringing her up and close out her transaction.

"My name is Wren, by the way," she says. "This might be my new favorite place, so you'll see me again." She winks as she takes her bag from me.

"It's wonderful to meet you, Wren. I'm Jo. I really look forward to seeing you again."

She gives a little wave as she heads out the door, and although she's basically a stranger, I feel like I've made a new friend.

***

Stepping into Frankie's house, I hear the sounds of laughter coming from the kitchen. Not wanting to interrupt their family time, I sneak to the guest room to set my stuff down. I pull my phone out of my purse, checking for notifications. Cole still hasn't texted me, but I refuse to think too much into it. This is all new, and I need to learn to go with the flow.

"Has he texted you?" I startle at the sound of Frankie's voice behind me. I turn to see her leaning against the doorframe with a smirk on her face.

"No, but he said he would text me after he got done with his route. I don't know when that is, and I'm sure he will want to go home first. I'm trying not to overthink it."

Frankie walks into the room and tugs me into a hug. "I know today was a lot. But I'm proud of you."

I pull out of the hug, meeting her eyes. "Thanks."

"He's going to text back, Jo. Now, come on. We made Indian fry bread." She heads out of my room, toward the kitchen, and I let out a happy sigh at the idea of some comfort food. Leaving my phone behind, I follow my best friend.

***

Dinner with Frankie and her family is always a loud, joyous occasion. There's always a lot of laughing and loud talking. Tonight it served as the perfect distraction. I didn't think about checking my phone even once. And I was again grateful for this woman who let me into her home and holds my hand through the difficult times.

After cleaning up the kitchen, Frankie aims a knowing look in my direction.

"What?"

"Have you checked your phone?"

"You know as well as I do that I haven't. I left it in my room so I wouldn't be tempted."

"Well, I'm super tired and really want to head to bed," she says through a fake yawn.

"It's not even 7 o'clock, Frank," I respond with an exaggerated eye roll.

"Yeah, well, my book is calling my name. And someone's phone is calling her name." She gives me a knowing look before heading down the hall to her bedroom, throwing her hand in the air in a lazy wave behind her.

I chuckle as I head to the guest room, but the closer I get, the more nervous I am. I sprint the last few steps to my room and close the door behind me. Leaning back against the closed door, I look to the ceiling, praying I have the ability to get through this, whether he texted or not. Finally, I take a deep breath, step up to my bedside table, and tap my phone.

I have one notification. A text from Cole.

I give a little squeal, climbing onto the bed and bringing my phone with me.

> Hey, darlin'. Sorry I'm so late. My route was long today. How was the rest of your day?

I smile so brightly that I know my cheeks will begin hurting if I keep this up.

> It was good. Frankie made one of my favorite dinners and now I'm just settling in for the evening.

Immediately, the little bubble pops up, showing he's responding, and his attentiveness warms my heart. The uneasiness begins to leave me as I begin to realize that this man has always seen me. He's always seemed to know what I need, and I'm sure, now more than ever, that he knows I need instant reassurance.

> Glad to hear it. So, when do you want to go on this date? And how set are you on coffee?

> Whenever you feel up to it. I don't want to be an imposition. And I'm not dead set on coffee. Did you have something in mind?

> Sunshine, you're never an imposition. If I had my way, we'd go out right now. I just don't want to push you too fast.

See, he just knows. The butterflies in my stomach kick into high gear. Before I can respond, he's texted again.

> But I would really love to take you to a nice dinner. How would you feel about that?

A vision of a candlelight dinner pops into my head, and I grimace at the idea, instantly afraid that it would be awkward, or I wouldn't know what to say. And like he's in the room, before I can really start spiraling, my phone vibrates with another text.

> Now, I know that sounds like it could be too much. But we don't have to go anywhere fancy. I just want to feed you. And if, at any point, you feel uncomfortable, we can leave. No questions asked.

All apprehension leaves my body. This man would make me feel safe and heard. Without understanding why, I trust him to take care of me. To know what I need or to read me in any situation. No more hesitating.

> That sounds great, Cole. How does Friday sound? I could meet you there or you could pick me up from Frankie's…if you're brave ;)

His response is immediate, once again.

> I'll pick you up, darlin'. For you, I'll be brave. Just tell the little menace to take it easy on me ;) Think about what time would work best and let me know before Friday.

I laugh at his jab at Frankie. Wouldn't it be nice if I found someone who could handle my outspoken friend?

> I will. Thank you, Cole <3

> Anything for you, Jo. I'll let you get back to your evening. Goodnight, darlin'.

I send him back a goodnight text before burrowing down into the covers on my bed. I don't remember the last time I felt this young. I'm giddy at the thought of seeing this man outside the confines of the store. My mind drifts back to that night at the bar. His close proximity. His breathy words whispered against my skin. My thighs clench together just as they did that night. I need this. I need to fall asleep happy after texting a boy. I need the butterflies to hit my stomach when I see his name on my phone. I need to be reminded that I am worthy and capable of passion. And I think Cole might just be the man for the job.

Chapter 16

"You belong with me."

Cole

Having access to this woman at my fingertips is a dangerous game. It's taking sincere effort to refrain from texting her all night. But I have to imagine that today was a lot for her. And I don't want to lose my chance before it even begins.

Later that night, as I lie in bed, I think about how precarious this situation really is. She's newly separated from her husband, and I know nothing about her or what she's gone through. I don't know what kind of trauma she's suffered or what potentially detrimental coping mechanisms she's formed. And for the first time since she asked me to go for coffee, I feel a pit forming in my stomach.

I have to acknowledge that I may just be a blip in her timeline. A small step on her way to figuring out what she wants in life. And despite not knowing her, I feel my chest tighten at the idea that I wouldn't get to keep her. But then a vision of her steely determination and her tentative smile flashes in my mind, and I know that I will be happy with whatever piece of her I get. And however long she allows me to have it.

***

Sadly, I have no reason to come back to the store before Friday rolls around. Jo and I have exchanged a few text messages here and there, but I'm more than ready to see her. I pull up to Frankie's address at six o'clock on Friday evening. I'm not nervous, but I am anxious just because I want this date to be enjoyable for her. I want her first experience outside of her marriage to be a positive one.

Before I get up to the front door, it opens, and she steps out. She looks beautiful. Her hair is down in loose waves. She's wearing tight, black jeans, tucked into black, leather booties and a deep green sweater. A black pea coat ties it all together. Her eyes meet mine, a shy smile on her face.

"You look stunning, Jo." I meet her at the front porch.

She tucks a strand of hair behind her ear before replying, "Thank you. You look pretty good yourself."

"You didn't have to meet me out front. I was okay ringing the doorbell."

She shrugs. "I happened to see you pull in and figured we would skip the awkward introductions." At that moment, the front door is flung open, and Frankie sticks her head outside. Seeing us, she steps out and closes the door behind her. "Spoke too soon," Jo mumbles under her breath.

"Did you think you could leave without saying goodbye?" Frankie calls. Jo just turns and stares her down. Frankie laughs before directing her attention to me. She gives me a long look, and I wait it out, knowing she has something to say. Anytime I've heard Frankie speak, she's always been jovial. She's always speaking through smiles and laughs. But when she finally speaks to me on her front porch, there is nothing jovial about her. Her smile disappears, and her tone lowers. "Be good to her. Don't be a dick."

That's all she says, but that's enough. This woman is fiercely protective over the people she loves in her life. I respect her a great deal, and I'm happy knowing Jo has someone like this in her corner. Knowing she will judge my response, I make sure my face exhibits the seriousness I feel when I reply, "I wouldn't dream of it, Frankie. She's safe with me."

Another moment passes, and Frankie nods at me. Then she turns to Jo, the smile returning to her face. "Have fun tonight, babe." They exchange a brief hug before Frankie retreats back inside.

Jo breathes out a sigh, meeting my gaze. I smile at her, trying to set her at ease. "That wasn't so bad. I was expecting a shotgun and a curfew," I joke.

She laughs, stepping down to meet me on the driveway. "Honestly, I'm surprised she went easy on you."

I walk her around to the passenger side of the truck, open the door for her, and help her climb in. I jog around to the driver's side, hopping in next to her before I respond, "Frankie doesn't need theatrics to get her point across. She loves you, and I know she'll have my balls if I don't handle this right."

Jo's laugh fills the cab of the truck. "That she will." She turns to look at me, a playful smirk on her face, as I begin backing out of the driveway. "Better not fuck it up."

I chuckle. "Don't plan to, darlin'."

***

The last few days we spent texting, Jo mentioned she didn't want to go anywhere fancy or stuffy. She thought she'd be more comfortable with casual. As I pull the truck into the parking lot of the restaurant I chose, I pray she meant it.

"Oh my god, I love this place! They have the best wings." She sits forward in her seat, beaming as she looks out the windshield at the building.

"Glad to hear it. I've been worried I chose somewhere too casual." I put the truck in park and shut off the engine. I get out, heading over to open her door, but she throws the door open and hops down as I reach her side of the vehicle. Her smile is wide as she walks to my side.

"This is perfect. I love this place, but I never get to eat here." Gently placing my hand on the small of her back, I start leading her to the door.

"If you love it so much, why don't you ever eat here?"

Her smile falls a little at my question, and she waits while I pull the front door open for her. Once we both step inside, she tucks herself in closer to my side as we maneuver through the cluster of people waiting for a table. I catch the eye of the hostess, and her face lights up in recognition. "Cole!" She grabs two menus and waits for us to approach the front. "I got your table ready. Right this way."

Jo looks up at me in surprise. I lean down so she can hear me as we're led through the noisy restaurant. "I may have called in a favor to make sure we didn't have to wait." She smiles when I wink at her. "The hostess, Sarah, is a friend of my sister, and she said she'd save me a table."

She ducks her head, suddenly shy. But we've made it to our table, and we each slide into opposite sides of the booth. I make sure to thank Sarah again as she sets down our menus and heads back to the front. My attention returns to Jo, and her eyes are studying me.

"Are you always this attentive and considerate?" she asks, warily.

My brow furrows with confusion. "What do you mean, darlin'?"

"You asked if I was okay with doing dinner instead of coffee. You agreed to pick me up at Frankie's instead of meeting somewhere. You agreed to choose a casual place to eat over something more date worthy. You called ahead to make sure we didn't have to wait. Plus, these last few days you've never left me on read. You've always responded to my messages and when you couldn't you always apologized and explained why there was a delay. You seem a little too good to be true here, Cole."

She seems to let all that out in one breath. And I'm honestly stuck, not sure how to respond. *How low has the bar been set for her?* I clear my throat, but before I can respond, she adds, "And, fair warning, I get very messy when I eat wings, so I hope you're prepared."

I throw my head back in a laugh. "Sunshine, you get as messy as you want." Then I grab the paper towel holder tucked to the back of the table and set it in the middle. "That's what these are for." I hold her gaze, keeping that smile on my face. I need to figure out how to make her comfortable.

After a moment, her shoulders tense and she says, "I never eat here because my husband doesn't like it. He doesn't like any foods that are messy that you have to eat with your hands." She rips off a few paper towels and arranges them in front of her before scooting the paper towel holder back to its original spot.

I take a deep breath. "Jo, I don't know what your marriage was like, and I don't need to know right now. You can talk about that if and when you're ready. But as long as you and I are doing...whatever it is we're doing, I will be attentive to you. Your comfort and having your needs met will be a priority to me. It's what you deserve. It's what any woman deserves."

She visibly relaxes as she stares at me, her eyes seeming to beg that I speak the truth. A small smile forms on her lips. "A girl could get used to this."

"Woman, you should already be used to this. But I'll fix that. Just give me time." I wink at her, and she blushes. *God, to see that blush touch the hidden parts of her body.* I shift in my seat, shaking myself of the visions of her flushed skin. *Getting ahead of myself.*

Our waitress comes over, and we both order wing baskets and beers. The conversation flows easily from that point on as we start getting to know each other. She's funny in an understated way, and I find myself laughing. But I hate the surprised look that quickly flashes across her face every time. She clearly wasn't appreciated, and I desperately want to undo everything that made her fit herself into a little box.

After dinner, we head out to my truck, and I wish I knew how to extend this date. But it's cold, and there's not a lot to do in January. Plus, I don't want to overwhelm her. Once we are both settled in the truck, she turns her body to me and shocks the hell out of me when she says, "Do you live close by?"

I swallow before I turn to face her. "I do."

"Can you show me?"

I hold her gaze for a moment and then nod before facing forward and easing the truck out of the parking lot. *This woman might be the death of me.*

***

My hands itch to touch her as I lead her up the front steps of my bungalow-style home. But I keep them firmly at my sides until I have to unlock the door and push it open. I hold it for her, and her body brushes mine as she steps past me and inside. She pauses, waiting while I set my wallet and keys on the table in the entryway. I glide her coat off her shoulders and hang it on the coat rack. Wordlessly, she follows me to the kitchen and perches at my peninsula seating.

I open the fridge to see what I can offer her. I was not planning on bringing her back here tonight. "I don't have many options, darlin'. Water or beer?"

"Um, I'll have a beer, thanks."

I grab two beers out of the fridge, cracking them both open before setting one in front of her and leaning back against the sink. Her eyes hold mine as she lifts the bottle to her lips. After taking a drink, she licks her lips before speaking. "You know, the night at the bar, when Frankie and I bumped into you..." She pauses, looking down to her lap, her fingers idly tracing over the beer label. "I couldn't take my eyes off your lips on that bottle." Her eyes dart to mine.

She's cracked a door, and I have to force myself not to throw it all the way open. Instead, I take another drink before setting it on the counter next to me. I step over to the peninsula, leaning down on my forearms so I'm inches from her face. My voice is gravelly, but I can't help it. "Well, that night, I couldn't keep my eyes off the way your body moves when you dance. I wanted to slide up behind you, place my hands on your hips, and feel our bodies move together."

Without responding, she stands. I'm hanging on a ledge here, desperate to see what she does next. She pulls her phone out her pocket, tapping the screen a few times, before a sultry song starts playing through the speaker. She sets the phone on the counter and moves around to stand in front of me. "Show me," she whispers.

Instantly, my hands find her hips, and I pull her flush to my front as we start swaying to the music. Her hands settle on my chest for a moment before wandering over my shoulders and back down. She bends back, just slightly so her hips are pressed against mine, but her hands now have access to trace down over my abs. She flattens her hands across my abdomen before sliding back up and pulling her body back against mine.

Her hips start to rotate, and a sharp intake of breath lets me know she felt my hard length against her. Her fingers claw my shirt as she makes another rotation with her hips. She peers at me from under her long lashes, her eyes giving away the desire she's feeling. I bring my face closer to hers, leaving plenty of room for her to maintain control. But she surprises me by tilting her chin toward me, bringing our faces even closer. So slowly, I ease in until my breath is tickling her lips. I watch as her eyes close, and she presses her mouth to mine.

The connection is instant. My hands travel up her back, pressing her closer. When I feel her lips part slightly, I let my tongue ghost over her mouth until she opens to me. My tongue caresses hers, and my hand makes its way into her hair, tugging slightly to move her head where I want it. She moans, and I capture it, breathing in her pleasure.

I break the kiss, spinning her so her back is to me, her perfect ass pressed against my aching dick. Her head falls back on my shoulder, and her hands wind up in my hair as my mouth begins leaving a trail of kisses down her neck. My hands travel up her sides and then back down to clutch her hips. A whimper escapes her lips before I hear the most beautiful words. "Cole....please. Touch me."

I slip my fingers under the hem of her sweater, feeling the warm skin of her stomach. I leave a trail of goosebumps in my wake as I caress her breasts. Her ass presses harder against my groin as I pinch one nipple through the lace of her bra. "More, please," she moans, circling her hips and arching her back. I skim my fingers back down her torso, before sliding one hand down to cup her over her jeans. She gasps before letting out a harshly-whispered, "Yes, please."

Still kissing the side of her neck, I work open the button of her jeans and slide down the zipper. I toy with the band of her panties, but another press of her ass has me sliding underneath the fabric before meeting her slick warmth.

I groan into her neck, biting down gently. "You're so wet, baby. Is this all for me?"

"Yes," she breathes. One of her hands dances in the hair at the back of my head, while the other loosely holds the back of my neck.

I apply pressure to her clit, and her hips jerk as she lets out a moan. I circle there for a moment before sliding my fingers down and gently easing inside her. "Jesus, baby. You're so tight. So fucking warm." I massage her inner lining with one finger as she slowly starts to rock against my hand. I ease a second finger in, pressing the heel of my hand to her clit. Her hips start a steady pace as she fucks my hand. "That's it, baby. Use me. Ride my fingers." She turns her head, pressing her lips against the skin of my neck. Feeling her breathy pants, I start to scissor my fingers inside her tight channel, pressing my heel harder, grinding it into her clit.

She cries out as her body spasms from the quick hitting orgasm, her pussy clenching around my fingers. The hand on the back of my neck tightens. Her grip is demanding, her fingers digging into my flesh. But I just wrap one arm around her waist to keep her standing and glide my fingers out of her, bringing them to her clit, working her through the pleasure. Once she comes back to me, I slide my hand out of her pants, bringing my soaked fingers to my mouth. She watches me as I taste the evidence of her arousal, and I can't withhold the growl that burns in my chest.

"One day, darlin', I'm going to taste you directly from the source." Her breath hitches, and she presses her mouth to mine, opening to taste herself on my tongue.

The song has long since stopped, the kitchen quiet except for the sounds we share as we make out like teenagers. Finally, we break the kiss, pressing our foreheads together, breathing heavily.

"Do you want to take this to your bedroom?" she whispers against my lips. I close my eyes, praying for the strength I need to say no.

"Tonight should be about you, Sunshine." She pulls away from me, frowning. I tug her back. "No, don't do that. This was more than I could have ever hoped for tonight. And as much as I want to take you to my bed and spend hours getting to know your body, I wanted to do this the right way with you." She melts against me again, and we just hold each other for what could be a minute or an hour. All I know is that I never want to let go of this woman.

She pulls out of my embrace, and I study her face, hoping I don't find any sense of insecurity. She gives me a lazy smile before biting the corner of her lip. "Bathroom?"

I lead her to the bathroom, kissing the top of her head before closing the door for her. I step inside my open bedroom door, adjusting my erect dick, which is pressing uncomfortably against my zipper. When I hear the bathroom door open, I step out, reaching for her hand and pulling it to my lips. I press kisses on each of her fingers before pulling her to the door. I help her into her coat before grabbing my keys. Reluctantly, we head to the truck so I can take her home.

***

I walk her to the front door of Frankie's house, readying to say goodnight. But she spins abruptly, pressing her mouth to mine in another searing kiss. I hold onto her sides, bunching the fabric of her coat in my hands so they don't wander. She breaks the kiss, whispering, "Thank you for tonight, Cole."

Words evade me, so I just press a kiss to her forehead. "Goodnight, darlin'."

"Goodnight, Cole." She smiles as she lets herself in the house and closes the door.

I make my way back to my truck, wondering how I got so damn lucky. This woman is like an addiction. I had one taste of her tonight and that is not going to be enough.

Chapter 17

♥

"And every time you shine, I'll shine for you."

Josephine

Frankie is sitting on the couch, reading her book when I walk in after leaving Cole on the front porch. She doesn't say anything as I ease myself down on the couch next to her. She stares at me a moment before her mouth turns up in a knowing smirk.

"Don't look at me like that," I reprimand.

Her face switches quickly to a look of innocence. "Like what?"

I roll my eyes. "Like you know something!"

"I know nothing," she laughs. "But I want to know."

I settle back on the couch, turning to face her. "He's amazing. Like, I'm waiting for the other shoe to drop, amazing." She listens attentively as I rehash our date, swooning when I tell her about how he made sure I understood that I would be a priority as long as I'm in his life.

When I tell her I invited myself to his house, she gapes at me. "You asked him to take you home? Like, to his home?" I just nod in response. "Damn, Jo. You're making all the first moves with this guy."

I laugh. "Yeah, that's not the last time." Her eyes widen as I tell her what took place in his kitchen. And I can't help the blush that creeps over my face as I tell her how amazing he made me feel, fully clothed, with just his words and his hands.

"And then he turned down your offer for more? What?!"

"He said he wanted to do it right with me. And I think I threw him for a loop," I shrug. At first, I had felt rejected, but then he had pulled me back to him, whispered encouraging words, and I believed him.

Frankie makes a show of fanning herself with her book. "Damn. Keep that man, Jo."

I wink at her. "I plan to." The words are said in a teasing manner, but I realize I mean them. I want to keep him. I'm not sure what that means, but I am sure that I want to keep exploring this thing with him.

Eventually, I say goodnight to Frankie and retreat to my room, where I replay the evening over and over. Finally, I reach over and grab my phone, typing out a text to Cole.

> Thank you for an amazing evening, Cole. I hope we can do it again.

> You bet your ass we're doing it again, Sunshine. I'm not ready to let you go.

His words spread warmth through my body, knowing this man might be as affected by me as I am him. We say goodnight, and I drift into a peaceful sleep, filled with deep brown eyes and breathy growls whispered in the dark.

***

The weekend passes in a hazy blur of happiness and flirty text exchanges with Cole. The following week at the store is busy. Cole brings packages a few times, and each time his eyes swim with the desire to repeat our dance in the kitchen. Tingles spread down my arm each time our fingers brush as we pass the signature pad. He always keeps it very professional since I've had customers in the store each time he's come in. But I am left a hot, breathy mess, wondering when we can be together again.

Wren comes into the store twice more. Both times we keep up conversation the entire time she browses. After seeing her the second time in the same week, I told Frankie about her and my feeling that she could be a real friend. Frankie said she'd spend more time at the store in the hopes of being able to meet her. I don't know what draws me to her, but I feel a kinship with her, and I am determined to woo her into my friendship circle. Having Frankie the last few years has really shown me how important adult female friendships are. And I just feel like Wren needs that.

Saturday brings a large shipment of restock items. They were supposed to come sporadically throughout the week, but shipping delays meant they all ended up at the store the same day. Cole brings them in on a dolly, and I heave a resigned sigh when I see it.

"This is going to take me forever to catalog," I whine.

Cole laughs. "Can you do it a little at a time?"

"No, I really need to get this stuff out on the floor as soon as possible. I've had people asking for some of it." I go to start pulling boxes, but Cole steps in my way with a huff, pushing the signature pad into my hand.

"You just sign for it, darlin'. I'll unload. Where do you want them?"

I smile and point to the corner behind my checkout desk, where he wheels the dolly and promptly slides the boxes in a stack on the floor. Taking the signature pad from me, he asks, "So, you're going to be working on this tonight?"

I sigh, "Yeah, I'll stay late once the store closes and at least get it all entered in the system. I can put it all out on the floor Tuesday morning when I get in."

"Alright, darlin'. Don't work too hard. I'll text you later." He leans down and plants a kiss on my forehead before heading out the door to the rest of his route.

***

Shortly after closing up, I'm unloading boxes when I hear a knock at the door. I glance over to see Cole holding a paper bag. He waves at me as I approach to let him in. He's changed out of his UPS uniform. He's wearing a pair of perfectly worn-in blue jeans and a Kansas City Chiefs hoodie. *Why does he look so good in everything??*

"Hey, what are you doing here?" I smile up at him.

He lifts the bag he's holding. "Thought you might be hungry, so I picked up a couple of burgers." My stomach takes that moment to let out a loud growl. He laughs. "Guess I was right, huh?" He starts to head over to the front counter, and I just follow behind him, once again amazed at his thoughtfulness. He starts unloading the bag, opening up a container of fries and pushing them towards me. I grab a few, inhaling the delicious scent before shoving them in my mouth.

"Oh my god, these are so good," I moan, closing my eyes to savor the flavor. When I open my eyes, he's stopped unloading the contents of the bag and is staring at me, his eyes blazing with lust.

"Sunshine, you got to knock off those noises, or I'm not going to be able to let you eat," he says, his tone deep and gravelly.

I swallow as heat starts to build in my core. The fries no longer interest me. I want this man. Before I can stop myself, I've stepped into his space, grabbed the collar of his hoodie, and pulled his face down to mine. I press my lips to his, opening and sliding my tongue over his mouth. He wraps his arms around me as his lips part, letting me in. Our kiss intensifies quickly, and his hands slide down to my ass, grabbing it to lift me, and my legs wrap around his torso.

Without breaking our kiss, he begins walking us towards my office. Once inside, he kicks the door closed and sets me on the desk. My legs part wide to give him space, and he tugs me to the very edge of the desk. My center lines up with the hard ridge in his pants, and I moan into his mouth when he grinds against me. He breaks the kiss, moving his mouth to my jaw, my ear, my neck. "Jo, I've been thinking about you like this for a week." His words are punctuated by the trail of kisses he's leaving. "Tell me to stop."

My breathing is ragged, my heart beating wildly in my chest. And the thought of stopping this causes a tiny panic in my system. "Don't stop, Cole. Please."

He growls as he pulls away, grabbing the hem of my shirt and pulling it over my head. His gaze travels, appreciatively, over my body, but I need to see him too. I start pushing his hoodie up his abs, and he takes the hint, whipping the hoodie and his undershirt over his head in one fluid motion.

I am transfixed by the sight of him. His golden-tanned skin molds to the contours of his defined pecs and abs. His chest is smattered with dark hair. Needing to feel him, I place my hands on his stomach, tracing each bump and groove before sliding up and tangling my fingers in his hair. He slides his arms around my back, unhooking my bra and letting it fall into my lap, where I push it onto the floor. He ducks down, kissing down my chest, over each breast, before pulling one nipple into his mouth. My head falls back in pleasure as he sucks and bites gently before moving on to the next.

I'm panting and in desperate need. He seems to know this and grabs hold of the waistband of my yoga pants, lifting me slightly to slide them over my ass and down my legs, leaving me bare on the desk before him. He squats down as he removes my shoes so he can finish removing my pants. Then his attention turns to my already dripping pussy.

"Fuck, baby." He leans in, inhaling as he presses feather-light kisses to my inner thighs. I lean back on my hands, whimpering as he gets closer and closer to where I need him. His breath is ghosting over me as he says, "You're beautiful when you glisten for me, baby." And then his tongue is dipping into my entrance, lapping up my arousal. I cry out as he runs his tongue up to my clit, pressing his tongue flat before sucking me into his mouth. He moans, and I feel the vibration before he slides two fingers into my soaking slit. I use one hand to keep me upright on the desk while the other clings to his hair as my hips start to move in earnest. "Good girl, fuck my fingers while I eat this pretty pussy."

His words set me off, and I'm crashing through an orgasm. Cole pulls his fingers out as he moves his tongue down, lapping every drop I give him. Before I'm fully through the wave of bliss, I tug him up to me, sucking his tongue into my mouth while I fumble with his belt. As I open his pants, he pulls his wallet out of his back pocket, pulling out a condom. He lets me push his jeans down his legs, and then I'm frantically pushing his black boxer briefs down, desperate to see him in all his glory.

His cock pops out, standing tall and rigid. My mouth waters, and before I know it, I'm leaning down, swirling my tongue over his tip, sucking up the drop of precum beading there. He groans and grabs the back of my head, tangling in my hair. He lets me pull him into my mouth once, twice, and on the third time I hollow my cheeks, sucking hard. He hisses before pulling my head back, his cock coming out of my mouth with a pop. Our lips meet again, and I hear the ripping of foil before his hot length is rubbing at the entrance of my pussy, which is clenching on air, desperate to be filled.

Slowly, he starts easing in, breaking the kiss so he can watch as our bodies join. I moan as I watch him disappear inch by inch until his pelvis is flush with my folds. He holds a moment as I get used to his size, but then he's pulling back and snapping forward in a hard thrust. I cry out as he grabs my ass, leveraging my body as he ruts against me. Thrust after thrust builds an intense pressure, but the lid won't pop off. As his thrusts grow more frantic, he lets go of me, leaning back so he can place his large hand over my abdomen. He puts pressure on my stomach as his thumb starts working my clit. "Come on, baby. Be my good girl and come for me." He flicks that tiny bundle of nerves hard, and I let go, pleasure lighting up my entire body. Cole moans into my neck as his cock pulses inside me, spilling his orgasm into the condom.

We stay there, him buried inside me, for long moments as we share slow, sensual kisses. Our hands wander over each other, taking our time now that our moments aren't so frantic. Cole finally pulls away, pressing a kiss to my forehead as he pulls out. The sudden emptiness is jarring, but my attention is on him as he pulls off the condom, ties it, and tosses it into the office trash can. He pulls up his boxer briefs and jeans, whispering, "Wait here," as he leaves the office, closing the door behind him.

He returns moments later with two paper towels, one damp and one dry. He gently cleans me with the damp towel, drying me with the other one. My body is jello as he lifts me off the desk, helping me redress before pulling me into his arms. He sits in my desk chair, situating me on his lap. "Come home with me," he whispers into my hair, his fingers drawing slow circles on my back.

I tilt my face to his, seeing raw emotion in his eyes. I kiss the side of his mouth. "Okay."

In comfortable silence, we pack up the food, grab my stuff, and head to his truck. I text Frankie to let her know where I'll be tonight, then turn my phone on *Do Not Disturb*.

***

I spend Saturday and Sunday night with him before he drives me back to the store to get my car Monday morning, dropping me off on his way to work. We didn't leave the house all weekend, basking in the glow of each other. I didn't even get any clothes from Frankie's, so I lived in nothing but his t-shirts all weekend.

We spent most of the time in bed, touching, talking. His promise to spend hours learning my body was upheld, and by the end of the weekend, I don't think anyone had ever been so in tune with my body. I lost track of the number of times he made me come, like it was his mission in life to bring me the most pleasure I'd ever experienced. *Mission accomplished.*

We made slow, lazy love, wrapped in each other, our whispered pleas and encouragement swirling around us. We fucked hard and fast as he bent me over every conceivable surface in his house. Even our attempts to clean up were thwarted, each time, the steamy water of the shower muting our blissful sounds. He cooked for me, and we ate in bed, our legs tangled together. We couldn't stand to stop touching each other.

Standing next to my car Monday morning, he kissed me, slow and deep. He whispered promises of more magical weekends in our future before helping me into the car and closing the door. We parted ways, and I drove back to Frankie's, wondering how it was possible to feel so much for someone so quickly.

Chapter 18

"Just wanna lift you up and not let you go."

Cole

I'm in love. I didn't know it was possible to fall so quickly. But here I am.

Being with Jo is like a dream. That weekend we spent sequestered in my house was a true gift. We talked about a lot, including what led to her decision to leave her husband. As she spelled out the blatant neglect and disrespect she received from him, I silently vowed to always show her that her voice is heard. I did my best to make her feel cherished in my space: rubbing her feet while we talked, cooking for her, checking in with her needs. During every intimate exchange, I asked for direction to ensure she was getting the most out of the experience. I took note of her preferences, how her body responded to each movement, and made sure she knew her pleasure was important to me.

I could barely keep my hands off her. Just having her in my space was incredible. But every time she'd get up and walk around in one of my shirts, my dick instantly stood at attention. When I kissed her head and smelled my shampoo from our last attempt at a shower, I felt this feral sense of possessiveness. I wanted her to always smell like me. When she was walking around out in the world, I wanted people to know that she was mine.

I've been with many women in my lifetime. Most have just been around for a good time, but I tried the relationship thing with a few of them. Nothing ever stuck. I never felt compelled to put in the work needed to maintain a relationship, so they inevitably fizzled out. With Jo, it's entirely different. I want to do whatever it takes to show her that we are perfect for each other. I want to show her how different life can be with a man who truly loves and respects her.

But I also know it's entirely too early to be thinking so long term. She's not even divorced yet, and the few times I've asked her about her timeline for that, she clams up, never wanting to talk about it. I always let it go, but it lingers in my mind, letting me know she isn't ready for what I want.

The last few weeks have been incredible, though. A few nights a week, we go out for dinner after work. Sometimes I can convince her to stay with me, and sometimes I drop her off at Frankie's at the end of the night. But every Saturday night, she comes home to me after she closes the store and stays with me until Monday morning. I spend all week looking forward to our weekends together.

I have today off, so I decided to grill some steaks for dinner and had planned to have everything ready to cook before Jo got here after work. But my sister called and needed my help, so I was gone most of the day. I'm just starting the prep when Jo walks in the door. I can hear her pulling out of her coat and hanging her purse on the coat rack, so I call to her, "Hey, babe! I'm in the kitchen getting ready for dinner. Want to help me?"

Out of the corner of my eye, I see her walk in. "Sure." Her voice sounds a little flat. I turn to look at her and notice her eyes give away exhaustion. She rolls up her sleeves to start washing her hands, but I beat her to the sink, washing the marinade off my hands before pulling her into my chest.

"You look tired, darlin'. Why don't you relax while I take care of dinner? I would have had this done sooner, but I was helping my sister for most of the day." I pull back, brushing a few strands of hair behind her ears.

"No, I'm fine. It was just a long day. I don't mind helping." She moves toward the sink again, but I stop her.

"Baby." I tug her out of the kitchen and start walking her to my master bathroom.

"Cole, what are you doing? I said I would help," she huffs behind me.

I lead her into the bathroom, dropping her hand as I start the water in the tub, setting it to the right temperature before pouring in her lavender bubble bath. I light the candle she put on the counter and turn back to her. "When you've had a long day, you don't need to help me cook, Jo. All you have to do is say no." I kiss her gently on the lips. She sighs as she relaxes in my arms.

"Thank you," she whispers.

I kiss her again before leaving her to relax. This is not the first time she's foregone her own comfort. We've had a few instances where she has not felt up to doing whatever it is I want to do, but she tries anyway. Luckily, I can read her pretty well, and I've stopped her each time. Hopefully, one day soon, she'll realize that she's safe with me. She's safe to say no or disagree or insist on her self-preservation. Until then, I'll keep insisting on it.

She walks into the kitchen as I'm plating the steaks. "Perfect timing, Sunshine." She comes up behind me and wraps her arms around my middle, laying her head against my back. I hold her hands, letting her take whatever comfort she needs right now. After another beat, she lets go, and I turn to face her.

"This smells amazing, honey." *I love it when she calls me honey.* Her attention is diverted to the food sitting on the counter, and I take a minute to study her face. Her eyes are brighter, and her smile is slight but genuine. Looks like the bath really helped.

"Grab your plate, baby. Let's eat." She carries her plate to the table and sits down. I grab my plate and the two beers I'd pulled out of the fridge, handing her one as I sit down next to her.

She's quiet as she cuts up her steak but moans when she takes the first bite. "Oh my god, so good!"

I laugh, loving how responsive she is to good food. "Glad you like it, darlin'."

She takes a few bites before setting her fork down and focusing on me. I watch her as she places her hands in her lap, preparing to speak. "Thank you for making me take a bath. I know you're trying to show me that self-care is important. And I know that I need to work on the people-pleasing. I'm trying. But you pushing me to advocate for myself is helping me. So, thank you." She smiles before leaning across the table and kissing my cheek. She settles back in her chair to keep eating her dinner, not expecting a response from me.

"You matter, baby. To so many people. You need to matter that much to yourself." Her eyes start to glisten with unshed tears, so I grab her face in both hands, kissing her deeply. Her hands grab my wrists, holding me there.

We break apart and each go back to our meal. Patience. She's asking me for patience, and I will give her that, plus anything else she needs from me. But part of me wonders if this is the best way for her to heal. I hate the feeling tugging in my gut that says she needs to learn how to stand on her own before letting someone else take care of her. Her husband never put her first. She never put herself first. I would put her first, but if I push her, am I much different than her husband? He wanted her to be a certain way. I also want her to be a certain way, but I can somehow justify it because I want her to choose her way. But again, if I play a part in this, am I just trying to mold her like her husband did? I shove these feelings down, wanting to be present in the moment with my woman.

Later that night, as she sleeps softly on my chest, I stare at the ceiling as I brush my fingers through her hair. My thoughts again swirl around and around. I want to keep her with me, but I also want to give her the best chance of living a full, healthy life. I drift to sleep knowing that it's entirely possible that I'll have to let her go.

Chapter 19

♥

"These chemicals hit me like white wine."

Josephine

"You're humming again."

I startle at the sound of Frankie's voice, turning to where she sits behind the counter at the store.

"Dude, it's like you keep forgetting where you are," she laughs. But she's not wrong. I've been lost in fantasy land most waking moments. Memories of Cole constantly playing on a loop in my mind.

"I'm sorry," I sigh, aiming a smile her way. "I've been dickmatized."

She lets out a surprised laugh. "You really are. But I am so happy to see it."

Before I can respond, the bell above the door jingles. I turn, seeing Wren walking in. "Oh my gosh, Wren! You finally get to meet Frankie!" I turn back to Frankie, my face alight with a smile. "Frankie, it's Wren!"

"So you said," Frankie chuckles as she steps out from behind the counter, walking towards where I've come to stand by Wren. "It's nice to finally meet you."

"Likewise," Wren responds. "I've been hearing that we need to meet." She smiles at us while Frankie eyes her for a second.

"Yeah, definitely Serena."

"Right?!" I exclaim as Wren just shakes her head with a laugh.

We spend the next few minutes chatting while Wren browses. But eventually, she just comes to settle next to us at the counter, and before we know it, we've talked the afternoon away.

"Jesus, I'm sorry. I didn't realize how late it had gotten. I'll get out of your hair so you can close." Wren starts to gather her purse, but Frankie stops her.

"What are you doing tonight? I stole Jo from her new man. I demanded a girls' night. We are going out for queso and margaritas. Care to join?"

Wren looks to me for confirmation, and I nod with a smile. Turning back to Frankie, she says, "Sure. My brother is watching my kiddo tonight, so I could have some me time. And a girls night sounds like the best kind of self-care."

"Perfect! Let's go!" We all gather our things and head out the door.

✳✳✳

"I'm so glad she came with us. I really think she fits, right?" I lean up from my seat on the couch, reaching to the table for my water.

"Totally agree. She fits our dynamic perfectly. She's stuck with us. We're keeping her." Frankie folds her legs underneath her, pulling a blanket over her lap.

Dinner with Wren had been so nice. We all chatted easily and shared our stories with each other. Wren is a single mom to a five-year-old little boy named Johnny. Her ex-husband willingly gave up his custody of Johnny so he wouldn't have to pay child support. She hasn't heard from him in 3 years. Her brother helps out when he can, but otherwise, she's on her own. I'm determined to earn her friendship and trust so she has more people in her circle to rely on.

"We should plan a dinner when the weather starts getting warmer. Grill hot dogs and burgers. Wren can bring Johnny so he can start getting comfortable with us."

Frankie nods. "Yeah, I definitely want to be able to help her. You can tell she's overwhelmed, and I don't blame her. Being completely alone like that, it's got to be hard."

My phone vibrates in my lap, signaling an incoming text.

> Hey, darlin'. Just checking in to see how your girls night went. Hope you had plenty of chips to soak up those margs ;)

I smile as I read his text. Catching on, Frankie snorts. "Guess that's my cue to head to bed." She smiles and pats my knee as she unfolds her legs and gets up from the couch. "Tell Cole I said hi." She winks as she heads down the hallway towards her bedroom.

"Goodnight!" I call to her. She responds with a lazy wave.

Chuckling to myself, I head to my room, hitting the call button on my phone as I go.

"Hey, babe." Cole's deep voice pours through my phone speaker, sending warmth through my entire body.

"Hey," I reply softly. I close my bedroom door and climb into bed.

"How was girls night?"

"It was fun. We ate too much and drank just enough," I laugh.

"Glad to hear it. Time with your friends is important."

I sigh contentedly. "It really is. Thank you for understanding that."

"Always, baby." His voice is soft and low. "I missed you, though."

"I missed you, too. But I'll see you tomorrow. What time should I come over?" Since we normally spend Saturday through Monday together, and Frankie demanded girls' dinner tonight, I promised to come over to spend Sunday together.

"Am I being too needy if I say, 'As soon as you get up?'"

Laughing, I reply, "Honey, you're not needy. I'll text you when I'm on my way in the morning."

He hums in my ear, sending a shiver down my spine and directly in between my thighs. "I love it when you call me honey."

"I'll remember that tomorrow when I have you in my hands." I pause. "Or in my mouth, or in my— "

He cuts me off with a growl, and I let out a little giggle. "Baby, I'm going to let you go. The faster I go to sleep, the faster I'll wake up and have you in my arms. Then I'll turn you over my knee for getting me worked up when I can't touch you."

The idea of his handprint, red on my ass, sends heat directly to my core. My voice lowers, and I purr in his ear, "Don't tease me, honey."

"Fuck, baby. You like the idea of me spanking your bratty ass? Grinding on my leg while I redden your bitable cheeks?"

My eyes roll back in my head. "Hmmmm, Cole." My voice is breathy, and I can hear his breath catch through the phone.

His voice is almost a growl when he speaks again, "Slide your hands in your panties for me, Jo. Tell me. Are you wet?"

My hand lands on my stomach, sliding my sleep shirt up and dipping under the band of my shorts. I rub my clit over the outside of my cotton briefs, already feeling my pleasure soak through the material. I move my hand underneath the wet fabric, fingers slipping and caressing my warm slit.

"Yeah, baby. I'm wet."

"Jesus, fuck." Cole clears his throat, but when he speaks, his voice is still throaty. "Make yourself come for me, baby. I need to hear you."

I close my eyes, moving my wet fingers to my clit. "Talk to me, honey," I plead through the phone.

"Fuck." I hear rustling, and then my phone is lighting up with a FaceTime request. I accept, and instantly, I see him. His phone is set up and angled, showing him lying on his side, facing me. His head is held in one hand, supported by his elbow against the pillow, while the other hand ventures south. One leg is propped up, giving the perfect view of his erect cock. His hand glides over the engorged head, sliding down to pump the length. This is, by far, the hottest thing I have ever seen.

"Let me see you, baby," he rasps.

I fumble the phone as I find a place to set it, angling so he can see me as I lift my hips to slide my shorts and panties off. He lets out a harsh breath as my fingers resume their exploring. I never thought I'd be capable of this type of sexual encounter, but he already has me so worked up, I think nothing of it as I slide two fingers inside myself.

"That's it, baby. Work those fingers. Pretend it's me fucking you slow and deep." I turn my head, lying on the pillow to see the incredibly sexy image of him, pumping his erection to the sight of me. I've never felt this desired. I mean, Cole makes me feel like the sexiest woman alive when we are together, but there is something entirely different about being apart and still feeling this way.

"Don't forget about that clit, baby. I would never leave it lonely. Give it some attention." His words light a fire in my core, and I sit up briefly to reach into my bedside drawer. I pull out the tiny vibe before laying back down.

"What do you have there, Jo? Are you going to let me watch you use that toy? Go ahead, baby. Play." My head falls back to the pillow, and I dip the vibe inside, getting it wet with my pleasure before moving it to my clit. My fingers resume their position, gliding over my inner lining like Cole would, ghosting over my G-spot. I turn the vibe on, and the minute the vibrations hit my clit, my hips buck into the air. I bite my tongue to keep from crying out.

"There you go, baby. Fuck, you're incredible." As my orgasm starts to build, I lock my eyes on his hand as he rapidly strokes his cock. I can see his fist squeeze slightly as it comes up over the head and then back down. Precum beads at the tip and is spread down his length with each pass.

I change the angle on the vibe as I turn the vibration up in intensity. "Come for me, baby," Cole growls, and it's as if he's hovering over me, whispering in my ear. My orgasm washes over me, flooding me with warmth as my eyes find his. As my pleasure starts to recede, I watch as he finds his. White ropes of cum spurt out of his cock, drenching his hand as he moans my name.

We both leave the phones on as we clean up and get settled back in our respective beds. My eyelids are heavy, and my blinks become slower and slower. "Goodnight, Sunshine," is the last thing I hear before succumbing to sleep.

***

The next morning, as I pull into Cole's driveway, his front door opens. Cole, barefoot, steps out wearing a black t-shirt and grey sweatpants.

My mouth waters as my gaze travels down those sweatpants, seeing the outline of his perfect cock. My mind automatically going back to the vision of him on the phone last night. I must have sat in the car too long, because before I know it, my door is flung open and Cole is scooping me out of the car and barreling back towards the house.

My laughter rings out as he kicks the door closed and sets me down inside, pulling me into a deep kiss. After a moment, we break apart, our lips curving into smiles against each other. "Hey, baby," he whispers as he kisses my nose.

"Hi." I smile up at him.

Grabbing my hand, he leads me into the kitchen, and my jaw drops. On the kitchen table, there are two gorgeous flower displays, clearly professionally made and probably costing a pretty penny. On the kitchen peninsula, a huge breakfast spread covers every inch of the countertop. There's fruit, bacon, sausage, scrambled eggs, waffles, homemade whipped cream, and mimosas.

Cole's arms wrap around me from behind, his head dipping down to whisper in my ear, "Happy Valentine's Day, Sunshine." He presses a kiss to my temple before I spin in his arms, wrapping my arms around his neck.

"I didn't even realize...I didn't do anything for you!"

Before I could freak out anymore, he pulls me into another searing kiss.

"You being here is everything I could want, baby."

I just stare at him, stunned by his selfless generosity and wondering how I could get so lucky to be the one he shares it with. He slides his hands through my hair, cupping the back of my head, tilting my head toward him. He leans in, and I close my eyes, waiting for a kiss, but then he says, "Let's eat." And he leads me to the table, sitting me down, and making my plate.

After we share the delicious breakfast and I fawn over the flowers, I lead him to his bedroom, where I reward his efforts, thoroughly, for hours.

***

Monday morning rolls in on the heels of a beautifully intimate night with Cole. My eyes flutter open, the room still dark, and I settle into the feel of him against my back. His deep, even breathing lets me know he's still sound asleep. Carefully, I reach to the bedside table, tapping my phone to see the time. Four am. I could go back to sleep for another hour, but instead, I pull my phone off the charger and start cleaning up my email.

I never look at my promotional folder, usually mass deleting from the browser on my laptop. But this morning, I scroll through to see if there's anything interesting. After a few minutes, my eyes land on an email from the financial institution that holds the mortgage on my house with Brad. The subject line is something encouraging a refinance. Instantly, I'm hit with a sense of shame. I'm here, loving another man, giving another man pieces of myself I should have been able to give to my husband. *My husband.* I'm still married and acting like I'm not.

I can feel the panic attack coming, on so I do my best to stay calm as I slowly slide out from under Cole's arm, heading to the bathroom as quickly and quietly as possible. Once the door is closed, I slide to the floor, placing my hands flat to the cold tile, trying desperately to ground myself. My ears are ringing, and my vision is tunneling. I can't quite catch my breath, but I try to keep my breathing even-paced. How have I let this happen? Since finding this happiness with Cole, I've refused to think about my marriage, compartmentalizing when I'm with Cole. But shoving my problems into a box and pushing them to the back of my mind is not the way to handle this.

Brad has texted me a few times, questioning how I want to move forward, but I've given vague answers every time, always implying that the store is keeping me too busy to focus on our separation. Always implying that it's on my radar and I'm working on it. But if I'm entirely honest, I'm not working on it. Just thinking about it overwhelms me, so I instantly reach for the calming balm that is Cole. He's become my crutch, my distraction. And that's not fair to him.

I move into child's pose on the bathroom floor, laying my cheek directly on the tile, my palms still flat on the surface. I'm being entirely selfish. And while this whole endeavor has been about me making decisions for myself, that doesn't give me the right to drag two men along while I decide what my life should look like. My breathing has slowed down, and the ringing has subsided. I open my eyes to see the tunnel vision has dissipated. I need to get myself together before Cole wakes up and sees me like this. I pull myself to standing, bracing myself against the bathroom sink before turning on the water to splash over my face. I brush my teeth and then quietly slip back into the bedroom.

I debate whether I should stay or leave but ultimately decide to stay. If I leave, Cole will be hurt, and my moment of panic shouldn't cause him pain. So, I slide back under the covers, scooting closer to the warmth of his body. He must feel me moving because he throws his arm back over me, pulling me tight to him. I let myself enjoy the comfort of being in his arms until his alarm goes off a short time later. Wordlessly, he switches it off before placing gentle kisses over my shoulders, neck, and face.

"Good morning, Sunshine." His whisper in my ear is gruff, his voice clouded by a nighttime of disuse. "Feel free to stay in bed. I can leave you a key to lock up when you decide to leave."

I turn my head to kiss him. "It's okay. I need to get up and take care of some things today." I smile at him, hoping he doesn't see my strained expression in the dark of the room.

"Okay, baby." He kisses me once more before heading to the bathroom to get ready for work.

***

Leaving Cole's house, I was determined to begin taking strides to divorce Brad. I needed to take back the reins and take control of my life and my decisions. But by the time I get to Frankie's and am sitting at the kitchen table with my laptop in front of me, all of my determination has disappeared.

The words are blurring on the screen as I'm overwhelmed by all the information I'm attempting to take in. Tears fill my eyes as so many emotions pass through my body. Shame, guilt, anger at myself for seemingly being unable to handle the decision I forced upon myself and Brad. Fear, sadness, heartbreak knowing that, if I can't follow through with this, I will lose Cole. Eventually, he will get tired of waiting for me to figure my shit out.

Slamming the laptop closed, I head back to my room, my head hanging low as I succumb to the fact that nothing is going to change today.

Chapter 20

♥

"Help me hold onto you."

Cole

"Where'd you go, Sunshine?" I reach over the center console of my truck to squeeze Jo's knee. Her head jerks toward the touch, pulling her out of her fog.

"Sorry." She offers me a sheepish smile but doesn't offer anything else.

"Something on your mind?" I'm usually hesitant to pry, not wanting to push her too fast, but she's been doing this a lot over the last few weeks. She'll be right in front of me, but not here with me, having disappeared down a hole in her mind. I can feel that I'm losing her, and it's taking everything in me not to grab hold of her and never let go.

Half-hearted laughter slips from her lips. "My mind is a chaotic mess. There's always something on it."

"Care to share? Maybe I can help." I want to beg her to let me carry her burdens, to unload everything for me. But there's so much we don't touch that I feel like I'm walking on eggshells. We never discuss her marriage or her plans moving forward, and I'm truly starting to wonder how long this can go on. She either has to let me in, or I have to let her go. The thought burns my insides.

"No, no, it's okay. It's nothing to worry about. I'm just a little tired." She takes my hand off her knee and intertwines our fingers, bringing the back of my hand to her mouth and pressing a kiss there. "Sorry, honey. Really, it's okay."

My focus turns back to the road as I drive us back to my place after a dinner date. And now it's my turn to spiral internally. It's like I'm having deja vu. Different variations of this same conversation keep happening. I know that Jo never felt comfortable expressing her true feelings to her husband, but I had hoped that I had laid the foundation for her to be different with me. Maybe I was naïve to think she would just bounce from one way of being to another if I provided enough safety. I was naïve to think I could help her without encouraging her to do her own work.

Maybe her husband was okay with this version of Jo. But I'm not. I want everything. I want her good, bad, and ugly. I want her happiness, her stress, her hurt, and her love. Jo is the first woman I've actually seen myself entering a true partnership with, but this is not partnership. And it can't be until she decides she's ready.

***

The end of March brings birthdays for both Frankie and Jo, who always do a joint birthday dinner to celebrate.

I pop my head into my bathroom, seeing Jo putting her earrings in. My eyes meet hers in the mirror. "Almost ready?"

Her face transforms into a smile. She's been lighter today. I can only hope it means she's started working through some of the issues she keeps from me. "I'm ready." She turns, placing her hands on my chest and leaning up for a quick kiss to my lips. I wrap my arms around her, holding her tight to me for just another moment. She wiggles in my hold before laughing. "Okay, big guy, let's go." I kiss the top of her head before letting go.

She ushers me out of the bathroom and towards the front door before grabbing her coat and purse from the coat rack in the foyer. I help her into her coat before grabbing mine. As I go to zip mine up, she grabs me, pulling me to her. Her hands find the back of my head and neck, gently guiding me to her level, where she kisses me, deep and slow. I feel her lips part, and I slide my tongue inside her mouth, our tongues tangling together. She holds me tighter, pressing her chest against mine, and I feel her balance shift to one leg as the other lifts and wraps around my hip.

I growl into her mouth as I grab her by the ass, lifting her up. Her legs wrap around me, and I walk until her back is pressed against the wall. I break the kiss and start trailing my mouth down her neck. Neither of us has said a word, but her breath is coming out in pants as her hips rock against me, searching for friction. I yank her sweater up and over her breasts, barely pausing to admire the black lace bra she's wearing before folding the cups down to allow her breasts to spill out. I pull one nipple into my mouth harshly, and she cries out, her fingers tangling in my hair, her nails digging into my scalp.

Her hips keep a steady pace, so I let her nipple go with a pop before pulling away, her feet meeting the floor. I don't let her get a word in before I'm unbuttoning her jeans and yanking them down to her ankles with her panties. She gasps as I spin her, instinctively putting her hands up on the wall before I yank her hips back. Her back arches, begging me for more. I fumble with my belt buckle and get my pants undone, not even pulling them all the way down before pulling my cock out and running it between her legs through her slick folds.

She moans and lets out a harshly-whispered, "Cole, please." I have no restraint right now, so I line the head of my cock at her entrance before sliding into her wet heat in one rough thrust. She cries out, throwing her head back. My arms wrap around her as I rotate my hips, grinding against her. Then I pull back, just to slam back in. Her cries echo through the foyer along with the sound of our skin slapping together each time I thrust deeper inside her.

I feel myself getting close, so I wrap one arm around her body, my fingers finding her clit, working her mercilessly. Her orgasm builds quickly, and moments later, she's spasming around me, her pussy holding my cock in a vice grip. I grab hold of both hips as my thrusts grow harder and faster before I find my release. My head falls to the center of her back as our breathing starts to slow.

I pull out of her and turn her around to face me. "Now pull up your pants, baby. We have somewhere to be."

She looks at me like I'm crazy. "I'm going to go clean up before we leave."

I put my arms up, palms to the wall behind her, bracketing her in. "No, you're not. You started that as we were walking out the door. Now you get to sit at dinner all night with my cum dripping from your pretty pussy." To make my point, I tuck myself back in my briefs, zipping my pants up and buckling my belt.

She doesn't move, so I bend down and gently pull up her pants, getting them zipped and buttoned. I fix her bra and her sweater, making sure her coat lies normally on her back. Then I pull her face to mine for another kiss, grab her hand, and lead her out the door.

***

We don't speak much on the way to meet Frankie and Parker, both of us lost in our own thoughts. Sex has never been our issue. It's been amazing from the start. But sometimes I think she uses that connection to lose herself in it. And I don't want our intimacy to be used like that. All these feelings are swirling in my mind, and I don't want to be upset at her for taking what she needs. But how can I not be upset when she won't share any other part of herself with me?

Dinner goes by normally, both of us finding ourselves and being present in the moment. Luckily, that openness remains between us as we head back to my house later, spending the rest of the evening just enjoying each other's company. But still, we don't talk about anything.

Jo's already sitting in bed as I brush my teeth. I can see her in the mirror, and I watch as she gets comfortable. As she settles down on her pillows, her phone vibrates. She picks it up, and it's like I watch the shutters close on her eyes. All her brightness dims. Her shoulders slump inward like she's trying to make herself smaller. I rinse my toothbrush and head to bed with her.

"Who is it?" I ask, climbing in next to her.

"Uh, no one," she responds, setting her phone back on the bedside table.

"Jo, don't do that. Who was it?"

She sighs. "It was Brad. Just wishing me a happy birthday and asking when we can talk."

I say nothing as she settles back in, pulling the covers up to her chin. She finally meets my eyes. "Can we just go to bed, please? I don't want to talk about anything right now," she almost pleads.

I hold her eyes for another moment before breathing out a resigned sigh. I kiss her forehead, roll over, and turn off the lamp.

"Goodnight, Jo."

"Goodnight, Cole."

***

Sleep evades me, and I spend hours staring at the ceiling as Jo sleeps next to me. It pains me, but I've come to the conclusion that I have to let her go. She has to be on her own to figure out what her next steps are. She needs the time and space to work on herself and what her future will look like. Maybe in time, she'll come back to me. But it has to be on her time. She has to be ready, and she has to want to be all in with me.

I finally doze in the wee hours of the morning, fully waking when the sun peeks through the curtains. Jo is still asleep, and I pull her close to me, allowing myself just a little more time to hold her. When she finally starts to wake, her head lifts off my chest, finding me awake and smiling softly. "Good morning, honey."

I don't answer her. I just tuck stray pieces of hair behind her ears, my eyes trailing over her face. Finally, I say, "Hi, baby."

A frown tugs on her mouth, her brow furrowing. "What is it?"

I can feel the sad smile form before I say, "I think we need to talk."

Chapter 21

♥

"I haven't met the new me yet."

Josephine

I think we need to talk. The words seem to echo through a vast cavern, despite being safely cocooned in Cole's blankets. *I think we need to talk.* My eyes close, resigned. This is it. This is when I lose him.

I lift myself off his chest, sitting upright and turning to face him. "Alright." I meet his eyes, determined to face this head-on.

He sits up and scoots himself so he's sitting with his back against the headboard. My eyes trail down his bare chest and over his arms, memorizing the lines of muscle and every shade of his tattoos. I finally meet his eyes, and my breath catches when all I see there is deep sadness, resignation, loss.

My shoulders slump, and my head falls into my hands, losing all sense of determination. I don't want to lose him. I don't want this to be happening.

"Baby," he whispers, gently pulling my hands away from his face. His thumb caresses my cheek, and his voice is low and gentle when he continues speaking. "You're not here most of the time, even when you're right in front of me. And you won't let me in. I've tried to ignore it, but by ignoring it, I'm just letting you stay stuck. You're not ready, and that's okay." He takes a deep breath. "It kills me to let you go, to let this end. But it has to. I have to. You need to be able to figure out what's next on your own."

He leans down, pressing kisses to my wet cheeks. *When had I started crying?*

"Jo, don't cry. It kills me to see you cry."

"I'm sorry I didn't think this through." His brows furrow in confusion at my words. "I'm sorry I started this so soon. I set us up for failure."

"Hey, shhhh. You took a chance and did something new. You needed that, and I was happy to oblige. But now you need something else. And it's time for you to find it." His large, callused hands cup my face as his fingers continue to brush my tears away. He presses a light kiss to my lips, and my heart breaks knowing this is the end. But I also know he's right. I need to move forward. But goddamn, this hurts.

We sit together in heavy silence for a few more moments before we both get out of bed. We brush our teeth, side by side in his bathroom, our eyes making sad contact through the mirror every few seconds. He steps into his closet to get dressed while I grab my clothes in his room, pulling everything on as quickly as possible. Stepping out of the closet, he meets my gaze before sliding his hand in mine and walking with me to the front door.

Our parting kiss is soft and lingering, fresh tears flowing down my cheeks. His eyes shine as he wipes my tears away, again. I take a deep breath before stepping outside, but once I'm out the door, I rush to my car, afraid to break down further. I barely spare him a second glance as

I pull out of his driveway, but I know he's still standing on his porch, watching as I go.

***

When I get back to Frankie's house, I send a silent prayer to the sky on the off chance someone is listening, asking to make it to my room without running into Frankie.

No one is listening, apparently.

She hears me before she sees me and starts talking as I head in her direction.

"Hey, you're back early. I wasn't expecting to see you until tomorrow."

I turn the corner, seeing the moment she realizes something is wrong.

"Oh, babe," she jumps up and pulls me into a hug as I completely break down.

***

"He's not wrong, I know he's not. And he was so sweet and gentle, I can't even be mad at him for dumping me," I attempt a watery-laugh.

"But it still hurts." Frankie hands me yet another tissue. We're sitting in my bed as I finish telling her what happened.

"And I know I've been pulling away. Everything with Brad is just sitting in the forefront of my mind, but I just don't want to deal with it right now, you know?"

Frankie's eyes bore into me, trying to read everything I'm not saying. "Why don't you want to deal with it? Are you...are you thinking about getting back with Brad?"

I jerk my head up, shocked at the direction of her thoughts. "God, no. Why would you ask that?"

"I guess I'm just confused about why you're putting it off. If it's weighing on you, why not just start the process so you can be done?"

"Honestly, I don't know. Anytime I've tried to start it, I get overwhelmed and just push it away and bury myself in something I feel better equipped to handle." My eyes drop to my lap, where I'm wringing a tissue in my hands. "But I know I need to stop pushing it away. I need to stop living in limbo and figure stuff out." Another laugh slips out. "Plus, I can't keep living in your guest room."

"Hey, you know you can stay here as long as you need. But I do think you need to talk to someone about what you're going through and see if you can find some resources for dealing with the divorce." Her hand covers mine, stopping the destruction of the tissue. "You're going to be okay, Jo."

"I know," I whisper.

***

Numbness is my predominant feeling for the next few days. If you can even call numbness a feeling. I'm on autopilot at the store, just going through the motions to keep things operating. My phone, which has been pretty active since my relationship with Cole started, has ceased all activity, which makes me realize how much I truly talked to Cole, even on the days we weren't together. His absence honestly hurts more than the absence of Brad when I first left. And I keep wondering, why?

Why do I hurt more for this man who I was only with for two short months? Make it make sense!

Wren swung by the store early this week and could tell I wasn't okay. She didn't push me to talk about it, which I appreciated. But she left me with a sad smile that just made me feel guilty for worrying one more person.

Frankie checks in throughout each day, and I keep telling her I'm fine. And I am. But someday, I want to be more than fine. I decided I get one week of wallowing in my feelings, per Lorelai Gilmore's instructions, before I put my big girl panties on and start the divorce process. One week. One week to stew before I start walking the road to *more than fine.*

Thursday is when the numbness starts seeping into panic. I have a box of restocks expected to be delivered today, and I am not prepared to see *him.* The moment I open the store, my heart leaps into my chest every time I hear the bell jingle. Every time I look to the door, expecting to see *him,* and every time it's not him, I feel both relief and disappointment.

Early afternoon, as I ring up a customer, the bell signals. Glancing over, my heart drops as I see Kay walk in the door. I turn back to the customer, thanking them, before turning to Kay to take the package they offer.

"Hey, my sweet Josephine," their words coming out in a soft croon.

"Hey, Kay. How have you been? Haven't seen you in a while." I try to keep my voice upbeat, but I know I'm not pulling it off.

"Pretty good. Happy to have my old route back." They eye me closely, like they expect me to bolt or break down.

"Well, it's good to have you back." I smile as I hand back the signature pad, turning to scoop up the package.

Kay gives me one last, long look before heading to the door. "Chin up, sweets."

As soon as they're out the door, I make a mad dash to the office, sitting down in my chair and putting my head in my hands. My heels dig into my eyes, desperately trying to hold back the tears rapidly forming and threatening to pour. *He switched routes.* I don't know how to feel about that. On one hand, I guess it's good that I get a clean break from him. His presence isn't going to be a constant reminder of what I lost. But on the other hand, is it so easy for him to just cut me out and move forward like we never were? I'm struggling to get a grip on my emotions, and I can't afford to break down while the store is open. I take deep breaths, putting all my focus on pulling air into my lungs.

I hear the bell ring over the door, and I sit up. *Now is not the time.* I stand up and head out of my office to greet the customer. Internally I just keep repeating, *You can do this. You're going to be okay. You're going to be okay.* I plaster a smile on my face and start helping the women who have entered my store. *You're going to be okay. You have to be.*

Chapter 22

❤

"These walls that they put up to hold us back will fall down."

Josephine

April passes in a blur of meetings and phone calls. Brad and I each hired divorce attorneys who communicated our requests back and forth. Neither of us wanted to make this harder on the other. We split up what we had, with Brad keeping the house. The day we signed the papers was the first time I'd seen him since I walked out the week before Christmas. It was sad seeing a life we built together dissolve. We shared sad smiles and a quick embrace before parting ways. I kept my chin up as I left, repeating my mantra in my head. *You're going to be okay.*

***

May consists of many therapy sessions, spilled tears, and exercises in healthy confrontation. My ultimate goal is to learn how to communicate my needs effectively. I want to be able to enter a new relationship when I'm ready and not allow myself to be swallowed up by the other person. *You're going to be okay* turns into *You know yourself, and you know your worth.* I also express my fears about actually putting all this into practice. I'm scared I am going to revert back when I start dating again. My therapist says this is how I know I'm not ready yet. But I will be.

***

June is when I finally stop squatting in Frankie's guest room. I found a nice townhouse, not far from the store, in a quiet little neighborhood. It's been fun to furnish it and decorate it entirely to my taste. Having my own space for the first time in my life is liberating. Sometimes I walk from room to room just basking in the knowledge that this is all mine. And I did it on my own. I get the same level of gratification for this accomplishment as I did opening All Eras.

My therapy sessions are still a weekly occurrence, but she says I'm showing serious progress. Opening my own store, standing up for myself and leaving my husband, and getting my own place to live are all accomplishments. And they're major. They're not small things. Once I was able to acknowledge that, other growth came easier. I'm still a work in progress. But I think that will always be the case. For now, I'm happy with how far I've come, and learning to stand on my own two feet has been an incredible lesson.

***

July is my month of planning. The one-year anniversary of the store is in August, and I want to put together a celebration for myself and for my customers. Frankie and I have been spending a lot of time hunched over laptops at my kitchen table, scheduling vendors, buying supplies, and searching for fun ideas.

Therapy sessions are now more upbeat. I'm excited about life and what it has to offer me. I ramble about my plans for the store, my long-term goals. Sometimes I talk about Cole and how I wish I had waited to start anything with him. If we had started now instead of 5 months ago, we might have been okay. But hindsight is 20/20. I haven't seen him or heard from him since the last time I was at his house. I respect the distance he put between us, but I do miss him.

***

The first weekend of August is the one-year anniversary of the opening of All Eras. We have a huge parking lot party with food vendors, a traveling bar, and lots of local vendors selling their items. Everyone was successful, and the store got so much attention. I was stuck inside the entire time, basically shackled to the counter; I was so busy. The store was packed from open to close. One of my quick glances out the window, I could have sworn I saw a large, familiar figure passing through the rows of vendor tents. But he never came inside the store, so I second-guessed what I'd seen.

That night, Wren and Frankie came over to my townhouse. They brought tacos, and we made margaritas. We sat outside on my back deck, laughing and drinking. Frankie had helped out at the party, bouncing between the store and assisting the vendors outside. Wren stopped by briefly after her shift to see how it was going before heading home to get a little rest prior to our dinner that night. We shared stories of customers and shenanigans we witnessed throughout the day. Their support continually fills me up, and I could not have better friends.

Toward the end of our evening, I let it slip that I've been missing Cole. I try not to bring him up because I don't want either of them to worry. But that night I just wanted him to be there. Frankie asked if I had tried reaching out, but I said I wasn't comfortable doing that. Wren just watched me closely before agreeing that I had to do what I felt was best. Maybe I'll be brave enough someday. Maybe I'll reach out. Knowing I run the risk of waiting too long and seeing him moving on with someone else is so hard to consider. And yet, I can't bring myself to text him.

My therapist says I'll know when I'm ready. The fear might not go away, but it'll morph into excited anticipation. After my friends leave, I lie in bed, basking in all my emotions. Happiness and pride fill my chest at how successful I've been with the store. The pride also covers all the growth I've experienced through working on myself. Pride gives way to determination. I'm determined to continue putting in the work mentally, emotionally, and professionally. But a small bite of sadness leaves a little mark on my heart, thinking about what I had. And what I lost.

Chapter 23

♥

"All along there was some invisible string tying you to me?"

Josephine

The end of August brings heat. Sticky heat. The humidity is so high, the air so thick it's almost syrupy. The air conditioning in the store is working overtime to keep it cool inside. I inwardly wince every time the door is held open, already dreading my electric bill next month.

When the bell chimes, and I hear the door open, I school my face into a smile before turning to greet whoever is walking in. But when I see it's Wren, I let my face relax. "Hey, lady," I exhale.

"Hey, staying cool?"

"Trying."

"Yeah, it's miserable out there." I nod in agreement before she continues, "I wanted to stop in and give you these." She passes me two envelopes. "One for you and one for Frankie. It's for Johnny's birthday party in a couple weeks. It'll be at my house with a bunch of his friends from class. My brother will be there to help me, but I was hoping you guys might come and keep me company. There's nothing like awkwardly interacting with other parents." She lets out a little laugh.

I open one of the envelopes, glancing at the date and checking the calendar hanging in my office. "Yeah, I can make it! I'm sure Frankie will be able to come too, but I'll give her this and have her text you."

"Thank you. It's going to be nice to have some adults there that I actually like. I love my brother, but I need my girls." She rakes her fingers through her hair, pulling it into a ponytail and securing it with the hair tie on her wrist.

I laugh. "I get it. What can we bring? What is Johnny into right now?"

"Nothing, seriously. Just bring yourselves. He'll get enough gifts from his friends."

I give her a stern look, and she laughs before replying, "Okay, fine. He's super into Octonauts and Paw Patrol. And he loves to color. Maybe some coloring books or something?"

I jot it down on the invitation. "I'm sure I'll find something."

She thanks me again before heading out. I shoot Frankie a text, and we make a plan to go shopping for a soon-to-be six-year-old.

***

"I should have taken a gummy." Frankie all but slams her car door closed.

"Oh hush, it'll be fine. You don't have to talk to anyone you don't know. Just stick to me and Wren." I roll my eyes at her as she rounds the vehicle, clicking the lock button on her key after I close my door.

"Fine. But I'm not talking to anyone. And I'm not touching any-one's kid."

"I doubt anyone is going to ask you to touch their kid, Frank."

"Hey, you don't know. Kids will talk to literally anyone. One could come running up to me with their sticky jam hands and ask me to help them with something. Or, and this HAS HAPPENED, they will try to touch my tattoos." She cringes before changing her voice to that of a child. "Oooooh, colorful. Me touchy!"

I laugh. "That sounds like a toddler. These kids are like five and six. I'm sure they'll leave you alone. Just put on your 'don't fuck with me' face, and I'm sure they'll be too scared to approach you."

"Excellent idea." I roll my eyes again as we start walking up the driveway to Wren's house.

Balloons and signs direct us to the gate leading into the backyard. Wren has set up different stations with outdoor games. A large group of kids is already bouncing around between them, yelling and playing. A group of adults stand awkwardly along one fence, trying to keep out of the way. *The other parents, I presume.* I spot a gift table that also holds a cake and lots of different drinks and snacks. Wren is busy writing names on cups and herding trash into a black bin.

"Hey!" I lean around her, setting my gift and Frankie's gift on the pile.

Her face lights up when she sees us. "Hey! Oh my gosh, thank God you're here." Her shoulders slump, and she closes her eyes as she smiles.

"Stressed?" Frankie asks as she takes the trash bin from her, resuming the cleanup.

"They're just little balls of chaos, leaving snack wrappers in their wake. My brother went to grab more trash bags because this is my last one, and I didn't realize it until right as the party was starting."

I grab her by the shoulders. "It's okay. We are here now, and we can help."

"As long as I don't have to talk to anyone," Frankie adds.

Wren laughs and pulls us into a group hug as she whispers a heart-felt, "Thank you."

I hear her back door creak open as we break our hug, and Wren turns, screeching, "Oh, thank you! You're my lifesaver!"

"Oh, shit," Frankie whispers, her eyes darting to me.

"What?" I ask, but before I can turn to look, I hear it. *His* deep chuckle.

"You know I got you, sis."

My heart starts beating frantically, like it's attempting to leap from my chest to get to the man who has held it for months. Frankie steadies me as I take calming breaths. I hear Wren tell her brother— *her freaking brother*— to come meet her friends. It's then that I turn and lock onto that crinkle-eyed smile I've missed so much.

Chapter 24

♥

"And your eyes look like comin' home."

Cole

She's here. And she's smiling. A shy smile, but still. She's smiling at me. And suddenly, I realize that my life has been all cloudy days since I let her go. Now I feel the sun beating down on my face. I close my eyes, breathing in the feel of that warmth.

I walk to where she stands with Frankie, Wren having already made her way to them. *Wren.* Clearly, she has some explaining to do.

But right now, my focus stays on Jo. I stop just a few feet from her. "Hi, Sunshine."

It takes her a second before she stammers, "H-hi, Cole."

Frankie's eyes dart from me to Wren to Jo and back. Jo and I have locked eyes, and nothing is breaking this. Next to me, I hear Wren chuckle. Frankie hears it too, and out of the corner of my eye, I see her head jerk in the direction of my sister.

"Explain yourself. Now." Frankie's face is stern, her tone demanding. This seems to shake Jo from the trance we've been in, and she turns to Wren as well.

My sister holds her hands up in the air, like she's surrendering. Her mouth tilts in a sly smile. "Yes, I know. But can we get through this party first? And once everyone leaves, I'll explain." When Frankie's face doesn't relax, Wren drops her hands, her smile melting away. "There's nothing malicious or nefarious going on here, Frankie. I promise. I would never hurt Jo." Her eyes plead at her new friends.

Jo pats Frankie's arm, saying, "It's fine, Frank. We can all talk about this later."

A loud screech interrupts the tense moment as a whirlwind child barrels into the back of Frankie, knocking her forward. Wren catches her and steadies her on her feet. Frankie shoots a look at Jo. "See?!"

Jo doubles over in laughter as the rogue child mutters an apology before running off to rejoin the game of tag. Frankie sneers at Jo as she continues to laugh before huffing a breath and turning to Wren. "You better have alcohol inside. I knew I shouldn't have been sober for this."

My sister smiles as she nods and starts leading Frankie towards the back door, Frankie mumbling the entire way, "I cannot do this. Too many children."

Jo's laughter has quieted, and we turn back to each other. She holds my gaze for a long moment. And then she pulls in a deep breath and starts talking.

"This may be inappropriate, but I'm trying to communicate more effectively, so I'm just going to take the opportunity presented to me and just say this: I miss you, Cole. I miss you a lot. And I respect your choice to cut ties and move on, but I need you to know that Brad and I are divorced. It was finalized at the end of April. I have my own place now. And I've been going to therapy. I've been working on myself, and I'm proud of the growth I've achieved in the last few months. But no matter how much therapy I've had, I keep missing you. I keep being sad and frustrated that the timing was all wrong. I keep wishing you'd walk through the door at the store with a package so I could tell you how sorry I am. And how, if it was you, I think I'd be ready to try again. But only if it was you."

She takes in a deep breath, her eyes darting back and forth between mine. My heart is racing from her words, and all I want to do is pull her in my arms and never let her go. Instead, I step closer to her and grab her hand.

"Baby, I didn't cut ties and move on. I had to switch my route because seeing you that frequently without being able to touch you, hold you, kiss you; it would have been too painful. And I figured it would probably be easier for you if you didn't see me every other day." I huff out a laugh. "You order a lot of shit, baby."

She rolls her eyes but lets out a little laugh.

"And I certainly haven't moved on. I've missed you every single day. I came to your anniversary party for the store, and it took everything in me to stay outside. But I knew if I went inside and saw you, I wouldn't be able to stay away anymore."

"I knew I saw you!" she blurts.

"I'm so proud of you, Jo. Seeing everyone there, all the vendors who came, all the people in the store. You've done something really special." I press a kiss to the back of her hand. She closes her eyes as she lets out a sigh. And her lips are just there, plush and wet, calling to me, begging me to take them in a kiss. Her eyes are still closed as I lean forward, my nose grazing hers. Her eyes pop open as she inhales sharply. We hold quiet, intense eye contact for another second before her lips crash against mine. I close my eyes, wrapping my arms around her as I pull her to me.

One arm stays wrapped around her waist as the other cups the back of her head, my fingers buried in her hair. Her hands cup the back of my neck, holding me to her as our lips part, and our tongues collide. Holding her again, feeling her love pour out of her, I know there's no way I can let this woman go again. She's mine, and I'm hers. And fate, *or a masterful sister*, has pulled us back together.

Vaguely, I hear the back door open, and Frankie's voice travels over to us. "Well, that didn't take long."

***

The party wraps up a couple hours later. Johnny has been consumed with all his new toys while Frankie, Jo, and I help Wren clean everything up. Once the last piece of trash is collected and the last table folded up and stowed away, the four of us crash-land in the living room, each nursing a cold beer.

"Alright, dude. You're up!" Frankie calls to Wren.

Jo snuggles into my side on the couch as I wrap my arm tighter around her. "Yeah, this should be interesting." She turns her head to look up at me. "Did you know?"

I shake my head. "I didn't even know you guys knew each other."

Jo frowns. "But I've hung out with her outside of work. I feel like you should have told me you have a sister with the same name as my new friend. It's not like it's a common name."

I think about it for a second. "That's a good point, but I don't know if you ever mentioned her name. Because I definitely would have commented on it."

"And you always just called her 'my sister' when you talked about her. I can't believe I never asked her name."

"Okay, okay. Can I tell my story now?" Wren interrupts. When no one says anything, she continues, "I knew Cole was smitten with you when he started mentioning you shortly after the store opened. So, when I checked out the store for the first time, I knew about you, Jo. I was curious, but I didn't want to draw attention to my brother's crush by introducing myself as his sister. Then, after you guys started seeing each other, I thought it would be funny to just surprise you both when he brought you to meet me." She pauses. "Then he told me that you guys ended things. And I didn't know how to tell you that I was related to him. I've really come to love and appreciate the friendship I've formed with you both, and I didn't want to lose you because a short-lived fling didn't work out." She winces. "Sorry, that was a little insensitive. I don't know what to call what you guys had."

Jo offers a small smile. "It's okay, Wren. But you should know that Frankie and I wouldn't have cut you off just for being Cole's sister. I would have figured out a way to keep you as a friend and maintain distance, if that's what I needed to do."

Wren grabs her hand. "Thank you. That means a lot to me. And I'm sorry I didn't tell you."

Frankie cuts in, "So, why did you ambush them both today?"

My sister lets go of Jo's hand, turning to Frankie. "At dinner, after the store's party, she mentioned missing him. It was the first time she'd said anything about him. You and I had been talking about how far she'd come and how we wished she trusted herself more to get back out there." She turns back to Jo. "When you finally brought him up, and you missed him, regretted how everything happened, I thought maybe there was a chance you were ready and just needed to see him again. Frankie didn't manage to convince you to reach out to him. And I knew Cole wouldn't reach out to you because he would never pressure you after putting the ball in your court. So, I knew if you agreed to come today, you guys would be thrown together." She lowers her eyes.

Jo breaks the tension by laughing. Wren finally lifts her gaze.

"Thank you, Wren. I needed the push." She wraps my hand in hers as she looks up at me. "I was ready. For you. But I didn't trust myself after mishandling us the first time."

I kiss her forehead. "You didn't mishandle us, baby. You just needed time."

"Time and a push." She turns back to Wren. "Thank you."

Wren looks at Frankie, who shrugs. "If she's cool, I'm cool." Then she throws Wren a wink and a smile.

"Oh, thank fuck," Wren exhales, throwing herself back into the couch cushions.

***

We all stay at Wren's for a little while, eating dinner and enjoying each other's company. Frankie and Jo hang back while I help Wren get Johnny ready for bed. We tuck him in, whispering happy birthdays as we turn off the light and slip out of his room.

Wren stops me in the hallway. "Are you okay? Are we okay?"

"We're good, sis. You cleared my clouds by allowing sunshine to filter back in. I'll never be able to thank you enough."

She blows out a breath. "I'm just glad you're happy."

"More than you know." I wink before we head back to the living room.

As we all prepare to leave, I tug Jo to my side. My lips brush against the shell of her ear. "Come home with me?"

She tilts her head back, pressing a kiss to my lips. "I was hoping you'd ask."

We say our goodbyes to Wren and walk Frankie to her car before heading to my truck. After we've climbed in and I've started the truck, she turns to me, a smirk on her face. "What are we going to do when we get there?"

I place my hand on her knee, sliding it higher up her thigh before squeezing. "It's been five months, baby. We've got a lot of time to make up for." I wink at her as her laugh twinkles throughout the truck.

"Good thing we have all night," she says.

I grab her hand and press a kiss to her knuckles before returning my focus to the road. *All night. And every night forward.*

Epilogue

♥

"This love is alive, back from the dead."

Josephine
One year later...

"That was the last of them," Cole says as he drops onto the couch next to me, his hand automatically going to rest on my thigh.

"Now we have to start unpacking," I say.

Cole groans, grabbing a pillow and crushing it to his face. I laugh before hearing a mumbled, "Can we unpack tomorrow?"

I pull the pillow away. "Fine. We can unpack tomorrow."

"Good." He lurches sideways, pinning me to the couch, his body landing between my legs to hover over me. He presses a kiss to my lips. He goes to pull away, but I grab his face in both hands, holding him there as I deepen the kiss. It lasts a few heated moments before he pulls away, both of us panting.

"I ordered food, and it should be here anytime."

I pout my lips, but he just laughs as he pulls back to sit up. I right myself so I'm sitting next to him, my legs propped on the coffee table in front of us. I turn my head, indulging in the handsome lines of his profile. "You sure you're ready for this?"

He turns to face me. "It's a little late to ask that now."

"Nah, nothing is unpacked. I can start taking boxes out to your truck." I act like I'm about to stand up, and he clamps an arm around my waist, keeping me next to him.

"You're not going anywhere, baby. You're home. And I've been ready for this since the moment I saw you." He nips my cheek and soothes with a kiss.

The last year has been pure bliss. Cole and I jumped back into dating like we never stopped. At first, we alternated where we stayed, spending some weekends at his house and some weekends at my townhouse. But eventually, we stopped spending much time at my place. Slowly but surely, my things started making their way over. My products cluttered his bathroom, my clothes started taking up space in his closet. So, when it came time to renew my lease, we decided it was time to take the next step. He helped me pack everything up, and we moved everything here, into *our* house.

We compromised, keeping some of my furniture and some of his. The rest we sold or donated. Now, every room of the house is a mixture of his taste and mine. And it fits together perfectly. This house is a home, which makes me realize just how much my house with Brad was just that: a house. I've been better about communicating and making sure my needs are being met. But Cole is so perceptive and knows me so well, I rarely have any complaints. On the odd occasion I do, we talk about things openly and make sure we give each other grace.

Once upon a time, I wanted to be more than fine. And now, I'm incredible. The store is doing great. My friends are strong and supportive. And I have a man who loves and cares for me deeply.

The doorbell interrupts my musings, and Cole jumps up to answer it.

I head to the kitchen but hesitate to set the table when I realize I don't know what he's ordered.

He comes waltzing into the kitchen with a bag of food in his hands.

"What did you get?"

He smiles as he unloads the bag, opening a container and holding it out to me.

"Wings, baby."

I smile as I grab the entire roll of paper towels and head to the table. He sits down before I get there, so when I approach, I swing my leg over him, straddling his lap. He grabs my waist as I pull his mouth to mine. After sharing a sweet kiss, I pull away just a fraction, my lips brushing his as I whisper, "I love you, you big beautiful man."

His nose caresses mine as he whispers back, "I love you, my sunshine."

Bonus Epilogue

♥

11 years later...

Cole

"These seats are so tight. Don't they know that big people exist in this world?" I struggle to get situated in my seat as Jo placates me with a pat on the shoulder. I look over to where she's comfortably settled in the hard, plastic stadium seat next to me. I huff in annoyance as she chuckles.

"It's just a few hours, babe. You'll be fine."

"A few HOURS? Seriously? This thing is going to be multiple hours?" I lean over Jo to where Frankie is digging into her purse, looking for God-knows-what. "Did you know this was going to be multiple hours?"

She victoriously pulls out the pack of gum she was searching for, popping a piece in her mouth before answering me, "I mean, the kid's graduating class is, like, 400 people. I assumed this was not going to be short."

I lean back in my seat, grumbling, as my eyes scan the room for my sister. I finally spot Wren walking up the steps toward our row of seats. Her eyes are puffy, but she's smiling.

She drops into the open seat next to me, letting out a long sigh.

"Doin' okay, sis?"

Her eyes glisten as she looks up at me. "I just can't believe we're already here. My baby is graduating high school. How did this happen?"

Jo leans across me to grab Wren's hand. "Father Time is cruel, Momma. But you should be so proud." She offers a reassuring smile. My heart warms in my chest. I'll never get tired of witnessing the strong bond these two have formed over the years. Jo changed my life, offering me a loving relationship I didn't think possible. But she also changed Wren's life. She brought strong, supportive female friendship to a woman who felt like an island more often than not. Jo, Wren, and Frankie are unfailingly supportive of each other, and it's beautiful to see.

"I am proud. But I miss my baby. And knowing he's about to embark on his own journey, out of my safe embrace, just scares the shit out of me." A few tears slip out of her eyes, sliding down her cheeks.

"Aw, babe." Jo pulls out a pack of tissues, handing Wren a few.

Frankie, never one to be left out, pops around Jo. "Hey, we said no crying. Get it together."

Wren laughs. "We said no blubbering. I'm not blubbering."

Frankie turns to me. "Switch seats with your sister."

"What? Why?"

"Because she should be in between her best friends and you. She doesn't need to be sitting on the aisle alone." She waves her hands in a *get a move on* motion, so I pull myself out of the tight seat, letting Wren slide into my vacated spot. I, once again, get myself crammed into the plastic seat before placing my arm over the back of Wren's chair. My hand lands on Jo's shoulder, now a seat away from me. I rub it absently as I listen to the playful banter continuing between the three women.

"You're a step away from blubbering, and this thing hasn't even started. Pace yourself." Frankie is swatted back to her seat by Jo.

"Leave the poor woman alone. If she wants to cry, let her cry."

Leaving them to bicker, I look to Wren, pulling her into the best side hug I can manage in these tight conditions. "I know it's scary, sis. But you raised him well. He's a good kid with a good head on his shoulders. Trust that you've prepared him for his next phase." I kiss the top of her head before letting go.

Letting out another sigh, she nods. "I know," she whispers.

Suddenly, the graduates on the floor all settle in their seats, and a line of educators cross the stage, signaling the start to the ceremony. We sit through the speeches, anxiously awaiting the diploma handoffs. When they start calling names, the tissues come out again, this time for all three women.

Johnny's name is called and our little section erupts in cheers and wolf whistles, going on so long they have to pause before calling the next kid's name. Johnny's eyes find us in the stands, his face blushing but beaming with a smile. He laughs before tapping his nose twice, a signal he and Wren have done since he was little. *I love you. We're okay.* A sob slips out before she taps her nose back to him.

***

The four of us stand outside the venue, waiting for the graduates to file out. Frankie stands on a stone bench, heads above everyone else, keeping an eye on the doors. Finally, she shouts, "Ooh, here they come!"

She stays still a few more moments before jumping up and down, frantically waving her hands. "Johnny! We're over here!" She keeps calling and waving before shouting, "You think I didn't see that eye roll? I saw it!" It's then I see Johnny's laughing face as he fights through the crowd to get to us. Wren helps Frankie down off the bench and we all pull Johnny into a group hug once he makes it to us.

Wren grabs his face in both hands, pressing a kiss to his forehead. "I'm so proud of you, kid! I love you so much."

"Love you too, Mom."

I ruffle his hair as his mom lets him go. He turns to me, and I pull him in for a hug. "Congrats, buddy. Proud of you."

"Thanks, Uncle Cole."

Jo and Frankie take turns hugging him before Wren pulls out her camera and starts getting the obligatory graduation poses. I take the camera to get pictures of the two of them, and then we are finally heading for the cars to leave.

"See you guys at our place?" Wren calls as she and Johnny start to veer towards her car.

"Sure will!" I yell back.

Wren waves and grabs Johnny's hand before turning and walking away. Frankie parts for her car, and it's finally just me and Jo. I wrap my arm around her shoulders as we walk to my truck. We reach the passenger door, and I go to pull away, but she wraps her arms around my waist and tips her head up toward me. I lean down and press a kiss to her lips. It's been twelve beautiful years of learning each other, laughing together, struggling, and loving each other. But no matter how much time passes, I'll never tire of the feel of her lips on mine, the feel of her body wrapped in my arms.

"What a day," she says.

I chuckle. "Yeah, what a day. I can't believe that kid is all grown up." I stare down at her for a moment. "Do you ever wish we had kids of our own?"

She ponders the question a moment before answering. "No. I like our life, just the two of us. And I got to love Johnny through each phase of his childhood. Being the aunt is exactly right for me." She hugs me tighter. "What about you?"

I smile. "Nah, darlin'. I wouldn't want to have to share my sunshine with anyone." I press another kiss to her lips before giving her a little love tap on the ass. "Now, let's go before Wren thinks we got lost."

She laughs as she climbs into the truck. Once we are out of the parking lot, I grab her hand, kissing her knuckles before settling our joined hands on her thigh. On our way to Wren's, we pass All Eras. And I send up a silent *thank you* to the universe that it ended up on my route, leading me to his beautiful woman and our incredible life together.

Acknowledgements

This book was infinitely harder to write than the last one. And maybe it's because the last book sat as an outline on my computer for an entire year. And this one just popped into my head, and I dove right in. Who knows the reason. But I struggled.

Mom, thank you for being my alpha reader. Thank you for letting me send you chunks at a time and listening to me complain about how this book was so much worse than the last one. You always encouraged me and never pushed too hard.

Caitlyn, thank you for the inspiration. And thank you for trusting me to write this story without ever reading it. Obviously, Jo is very loosely based on you. Store owner. People pleaser. Strong woman realizing her own strength. I was at the store one time when the UPS man brought a box of books, and I instantly had an idea for a story about a woman who eventually falls for the UPS driver. I had a lot to fill in around that concept, and I know you were nervous. But this book is not your story. Your story is real and is inspiring. I hope you are as proud of yourself as I am of you. You can do it all. You're an attentive wife, a loving mother, a kickass business owner, an incredible friend. You are so much more than words on a page. I started writing this and decided you didn't get to read it until it was finished because I

didn't want you to freak out. I hope you're not freaking out right now
;)

Nic and Caitlin, thank you for being my beta readers again. Your input is always super helpful and makes me a better writer. The book is better because of you.

Jaquelyn, thank you for taking me on again and editing another book for me. I can be difficult and over communicative, so thank you for putting up with me.

To the readers who came back to me, thank you. If you read A Soul Seen and came back to read this one, you have no idea how much I appreciate you. I hope I didn't let you down. I really switched up the genre, so I hope there was no whiplash.

To any new readers, thank you, too! I hope you enjoyed my dip into contemporary romance. Your support means the world.

When I wrote my first book, my son (who was seven at the time) made sure he told anyone who entered my house, "My mom wrote a book!" He would grab the book off my shelf and hand it to everyone, proudly exclaiming, "She wrote ALL of that!" Connor, when you're old enough, I'll let you read this page and hope you never decided to read the rest. Thank you for being you. You are such a kind, sensitive, caring little boy, and I am so very proud of you. I can't wait to see you continue to grow and evolve. I can't wait to see who you decide to be in this life. No matter what, I am your biggest supporter and will always be here, cheering you on.

And finally to my street team, Lola's Legion. We are small, but we are mighty! The support and encouragement I've gotten from you guys seriously blows my mind. The fact that you choose to spend a little of your free time every day helping to hype a baby indie author is truly so amazing. There aren't enough words in any language to explain how grateful and appreciative I am of each and every one of you. Thank you for helping to hype this book and for sticking with me on the next one!

About the author

Lola B. Marie was born and raised in the Midwest. She's an avid Chiefs fan, a terribly competitive fantasy football player, and a romance reader. She lives with her husband, son, dogs, and cat. All the pets are boys, and she doesn't mind being outnumbered. When she isn't writing or with her family, you can find her hanging at Bedpost Books, her favorite locally-owned bookstore in the Midwest. She's also usually listening to one of a hundred podcasts while drinking Dr. Pepper and eating some sort of gummy candy.

As a typical pissy Pisces, she's also a dreamer who never expected one of her dreams to come true. Writing was always something she enjoyed, but she never thought she'd write something to completion. And now she's a published author. Live your dreams, kids. They're possible if you want them to be.